Wine Country Killer

A Cedar bay Cozy Mystery - Book 15

BY

DIANNE HARMAN

Published by: Dianne Harman

www.dianneharman.com

Interior, cover design and website by
Vivek Rajan

ISBN: 9781790297054

CONTENTS

ACKNOWLEDGMENTS

It takes a lot of people to get a book to the point where it's ready to be published. Editors, copy editors, cover designers, formatters, researchers, etc. Each book is a collaborative effort on the part of all of these different people, and I'm grateful to have people I can totally rely on. Vivek, Connie, and Meghan, thank you!

Those are the people who help me with the nuts and bolts of producing a book, but it's my family that sustains me and gives me constant encouragement. Michelle, Lamine, Mike, Noelle, Chloe, and Liam, thanks. And I would be totally remiss without a huge thank you to my best friend, my in-house editor, and my husband, Tom!

And of course, a big thanks to all my loyal readers. I thoroughly enjoyed writing this book, and I hope you enjoy the read just as much. It's a little different from the other cozy mysteries that I've written, but I think it's one of my best. As always, I welcome your feedback, and if you're so inclined, a review is always appreciated.

Again, thanks to all of you for everything you do to make my books bestsellers!

.

PROLOGUE

Ethan Morris looked around the patio area of the Broadmoor Hotel in Colorado Springs where the biannual meeting of the exclusive Brotherhood of the Knights of Wine was being held. He marveled at the spectacular surroundings of the historic and majestic hotel. The Broadmoor was internationally known as one of the finest hotels in the United States. It opened in 1918 and had a long history of providing accommodations to the rich and famous of the world.

The Broadmoor was on a par with other famous hotels in America such as The Homestead in Hot Springs, Virginia, The Greenbrier in West Virginia, and the Hotel Del Coronado in San Diego. Situated adjacent to the Front Range of the picturesque Colorado Rockies, it provided luxurious amenities to its guests that were entirely compatible with its five-star rating.

As he sat in one of the lounge chairs on the patio, Ethan admired the twinkling lights that lit up the spacious outdoor area. The center of attention was a huge rock fireplace that held a roaring fire made with logs the size of tree trunks, its warmth extending as far as the edge of the patio and beyond. Comfortable chairs and lounges were scattered in seating areas on the patio along with high top cocktail tables surrounded by upholstered stools. Sitting there, he noticed that he felt slightly dizzy, and he wondered if it was being caused by the large amount of wine he'd consumed or the effects of the high altitude for which Colorado was so famous. It was a little after 8:00

p.m. and he'd been drinking wine continuously since 5:00 p.m., so he was inclined to think it was the wine.

No one could complain about the quality of the wine that was flowing freely. In fact, as soon as you finished a glass of wine, you were free to step up to one of the tables and help yourself to another one. The outpouring of all the free wine you wanted to drink was courtesy of the Sonoma, California vintners who had been chosen to provide the wine for the meeting.

The biannual meeting of the Brotherhood of the Knights of Wine was considered by members of the wine industry to be the most prestigious wine tasting event in the country. As such, only the best of the best vineyards was fortunate enough to have their wines poured at one of the Brotherhood's meetings. Prior to every meeting, the Executive Committee of the Brotherhood screened the applications of vintners from around the world before deciding which wines would receive the honor of being featured at a meeting of the Brotherhood.

The meeting at the Broadmoor featured the wines of Sonoma, and the best vintners from that area of California willingly shared their latest releases with the members of the Brotherhood. All around him wine connoisseurs spoke of the bloom of one wine, or whether or not the chardonnay had too much of an "oaky" taste and how incredible the smell or bouquet of another wine was.

Ethan smiled as several members of the Brotherhood stopped by to congratulate him for becoming a new member. He was wearing the prestigious red robe (which represented red wines) with a white braided neckpiece (which represented white wines). Earlier that evening, along with five other people, he had been inducted into the Brotherhood.

At the conclusion of the installation ceremony, the president of the Brotherhood had lightly touched Ethan on each shoulder with a sabrage, a small sword dating back to the days of the Napoleonic Wars, that was used to open champagne bottles. He then presented Ethan with his own personalized tasting cup, his name engraved on it in gold lettering. The cup was attached to a heavy gold chain which he wore around his neck.

The fee to join the Brotherhood's exclusive group was $10,000, and that was just the starting point. The Brotherhood assumed that anyone who could afford to join could easily pay the expenses involved in traveling to the biannual meetings, such as plane fares and staying at the most exclusive hotels and resorts in the United States. True to form, the nightly room rate at the Broadmoor was $950 a night. It went without saying that members of the Brotherhood were expected to buy several cases of wine at the biannual meetings to support the vintners who hosted the wine tastings.

There were a number of workshops scheduled for the next day, but Ethan doubted if he'd be able to attend given the fact that he'd had far more to drink tonight than he should have. Even though the appetizers such as ahi tuna ceviche, lobster ravioli, and the hangar steak slices with caramelized onions had been fabulous, he was hungry for a good old hamburger.

When he'd driven in from Denver that afternoon, he'd noticed a McDonalds not too far away, and as well-known as the Broadmoor was for its fine dining, he craved a hamburger and fries from there. He gulped down the glass of wine that he'd poured a few moments earlier. *No sense wasting good wine,* he thought to himself, and left the patio tasting area. He weaved his way across the patio and took an elevator up to his room with the idea in mind that he'd change his clothes and sneak off the premises, so he could go to the nearby McDonalds and get a good old-fashioned hamburger with fries.

His room was elegant, with its balcony and fireplace, but unfortunately due to his alcohol consumption, it was spinning slightly when he entered it. He slowly and carefully sat down on the bed as he began to take off his ceremonial robe. The room had cost far more than he'd planned on spending, but he didn't want to appear like he didn't have a lot of money, and since all of the reservations had to be made through the Brotherhood, when the secretary had suggested a room with upgraded amenities, he'd eagerly said yes, a decision he knew he'd regret when he got his monthly credit card statement.

After he'd taken off his robe, Ethan changed into jeans and a t-shirt. He thought about calling Uber and having a driver take him to McDonalds, but he could just imagine what an Uber driver would think about someone getting a ride from the Broadmoor to a McDonalds. It was a foolish reason for making an unwise choice, and one he would regret later. Instead, he tested his sobriety by seeing if he could walk a straight line from the bathroom to the far side of the balcony. *Piece of cake.* He'd drive.

The McDonalds he'd seen when he drove to the hotel earlier in the day was less than a mile from the hotel. A broad well-lighted street led directly from the hotel entrance to the McDonalds. He was cruising along the street, doing quite well he thought, considering how much he had had to drink, when he looked down at his speedometer and realized he was going 55 mph in a 25 mph zone.

He was in the process of slowing down when he saw the Golden Arches of McDonalds coming up fast on his right. He yanked the steering wheel to the right, trying with some difficulty to line his car up with the driveway entrance. He missed the entrance and bounced up over the adjoining curb, coming down with a small crash in the center of the McDonald's parking lot. The only problem was that he was traveling at a speed of 40 mph, far too fast for the crowded parking lot which was filled with parked cars and customers coming and going from the main entrance of the restaurant.

He saw the drive-through lane ahead on his left and headed for it, but he never saw the woman with two small children who had gotten out of their car and were walking across the parking lot. He heard the sounds of their bodies as they struck his car with a sickening thud, and even in his befuddled state, he realized something very bad had happened. The screams of bystanders confirmed his fears. At the very least, he knew he'd be arrested for drunk driving and who knew what else.

Ethan already had two previous DUI arrests, and if he got a third, it would mean he'd not only lose his driver's license, but he'd probably go to jail. Making a spur of the moment decision, he swerved out of the drive-through lane, drove through the parking lot to the back exit, and merged into traffic on the busy street he'd been on when he drove to the McDonalds from the Broadmoor.

A half hour later he was back at the Broadmoor, packed, and standing just outside the front entrance doors, waiting for a shuttle van to take him to the Denver airport. His heart was pounding in his chest and his throat was dry, but there was no time for another drink to ease his rising panic. He'd seen the breaking news on the television in his room about a woman and her two children being killed by a hit-and-run driver in the parking lot of a local McDonald's restaurant. According to the broadcast announcer, the driver had fled the scene of the accident and no one had thought to get the license plate number of the car. Paramedics had rushed to the scene of the accident, but it was too late. The woman and her two children were pronounced dead by them.

*****

Several days later the police were called by the security detail at the Broadmoor Hotel about a car that had been abandoned in the hotel's parking garage. When the police checked with the rental car company, they found out it had been rented to Ethan Morris. There was front end damage to the car, a broken right front headlight, and bloodstains on the right front fender of the car.

Laboratory tests concluded that the bloodstains matched the blood types of the three hit-and-run victims. Further investigation by the police revealed that Ethan Morris's name was listed on a passenger manifest for a flight to Mexico City from Denver at 2:00 a.m. in the early morning hours after the accident occurred.

That was the last time the authorities or anyone else ever heard anything about Ethan Morris. He simply vanished into the sometimes lawless and corrupt country of Mexico, never again to be seen. When three people have been killed in a hit-and-run accident, the options are rather limited for the perpetrator of such a crime.

Apparently, for Ethan Morris, getting lost in Mexico seemed like the best option.

CHAPTER ONE

"Mike, I can't tell you how much I'm looking forward to this coming week. It's a first for us. Staying at home, both of us off work, sleeping in, no murders to solve, just enjoying each other and Rebel, Lady, and Skyy. I don't know what heaven's like, but this may be as close to it as I'll ever get." Kelly Reynolds smiled as she looked over her coffee cup at her husband.

"I hear you loud and clear, and I couldn't agree more. I intend to do a couple of things around the house, sleep, eat, and maybe play a round or two of golf. I'm not sure it gets much better than this. I mean it, Kelly, look outside." Her husband motioned to the window. "The sun's shining on the water in the bay, making it look like a million little diamonds are sparkling out there. Yep, this is nirvana, and it's right in our own back yard."

He stood up and walked over to the kitchen counter to get more coffee and another muffin. Kelly looked at him wryly and said, "My love, if you keep eating those muffins, you won't be able to get your sheriff's uniform on when you go back to work next week. May be the first time in the history of Oregon's Beaver County Sheriff's Department that a sheriff had to resign because he'd outgrown his uniform."

"Kelly, cut me a little slack here. I'm on my first day of vacation. I'm allowed an extra muffin or two." Mike eyed the offending delicacies with gusto.

"One more muffin, Sheriff, and that's it. If you have any more you'll be back in bed for the rest of the day with a food coma. That doesn't seem like a particularly good way to start a vacation."

"This is the last one, I promise," he said as he selected the biggest muffin in the tin. He sat back down and took a big bite of it. At that moment his cell phone rang. He picked it up and said with a full mouth, "Sheriff Reynolds here." He took a big drink from his coffee cup to help him swallow the muffin. He listened for a moment and then he said, "Of course I remember you, Sheriff Dawson."

He looked over at Kelly who had raised an eyebrow, well remembering when she and Mike had helped Sheriff Ted Dawson the time they'd been visiting Sonoma, California for a reunion with Kelly's daughter, Julia, and her husband, Brad. Unfortunately Julia and Brad had to leave early because one of their daughters was ill. After they'd left, Kelly and Mike had spent the remainder of their time in Sonoma successfully searching for the person responsible for murdering Angela Lucci by pushing her into a wine vat.

Mike continued to listen to the sheriff and then he said, "I'm sure you understand that I need to talk to Kelly about this. We're taking this week off, a vacation for us, and I have to tell you that looking for a serial killer was really not on our to-do list. I'll get back to you shortly." He ended the call and looked at her.

Kelly frowned. "Okay, Mike, let's have it. Knowing you, I'd bet we're off to Sonoma to look for a serial killer."

"Only if you're on board, Kelly, and I mean it. Here's what Dawson told me. Four vintners have been murdered in the Sonoma area over the past six months. All of them were murdered while they were doing something with wine, like working in their vineyard, or the tasting room, etcetera. The first was six months ago, the second was three months ago, the third was a month ago and the last one was two weeks ago. He's concerned it's a serial killer, and it looks like the killer is stepping up the pace."

"Why did he call you?"

"Actually, he called both of us. He feels we were the ones who figured out who murdered Angela Lucci, and he's right, we did. He'd like to hire us for a week and see what we can come up with. He says he has a little money for things like that in his budget. Wish I had something like that in my budget, but that's neither here nor there."

"How are we supposed to help?" Kelly asked.

"Dawson wants us to act as a set of fresh eyes in the investigation. His department has had no luck catching the serial killer. This person seems to be targeting wine makers exclusively, but that's the only nexus. He says the wine growers are up in arms about it and scared to death one of them will be the killer's next victim. Can't say I blame them."

"Well, I love the Sonoma area, but I don't know how we could be of much help if his department is out of clues. Anyway, this is the tail end of the tourist season. We'd never be able to find a place to stay."

"Looks like that's taken care of. One of the vintners is a good friend of Sheriff Dawson's. She has a guest cottage which is on her winery property next to her home. She told him if he could find someone to help, they could stay with her. Oh, and one of the vintners has a private plane who will pick us up in Portland. Dawson said that way I can bring my own gun, and he remembered that you had a dog that had helped solve murders. He suggested we could bring Rebel with us on the private plane."

"Sounds like he's thought of everything," Kelly said, with a sigh of resignation. "Rebel's never flown. Hope he doesn't get airsick."

"Me, too. I take that statement as you being okay with us going there."

"Mike, was there ever any doubt?" she asked with a knowing look on her face.

"Not really," he said as he picked up his phone.

CHAPTER TWO

Riccardo Neri looked at his reflection in the mirror and smiled as he finished shaving. It was getting close to wine crush time, and he was sure this year would be the year his label, Neri Vineyards, would receive a prestigious award for the reserve chardonnay he was releasing in a few months. He was a modest man, but his daily sampling of the grapes from his vineyard made him think the award would be his.

Every day for the past several weeks he'd walked through the rows of grapes in his vineyard, plucking a single grape from first one vine and then another one from a different vine. The taste and texture of the test grapes had been beyond anything he'd ever produced before.

He only wished the reserve chardonnay that would be produced from this year's harvest had been available two years earlier when the wines of Sonoma had been featured at the Broadmoor Hotel during the Brotherhood of the Knights of Wine biannual meeting. Wine connoisseurs from throughout the world had been there, and he knew they probably would have bought every case of wine he was going to make with this year's crop of grapes.

Also, being an eternal optimist, he was sure that even without that prestigious springboard, when Wine Spectator magazine heard about his new release, they would write an article about it. He was certain the wine he was about to produce would be amazingly delicious, and would be sold out soon after the magazine article was published.

It was quiet in his house. His wife, Marta, was in Los Angeles, visiting their daughter, Valentina, at the University of Southern California. It was parents' weekend at her sorority, but Riccardo had told Marta he couldn't go. It was too close to the wine crush time and a day or two could make all difference in the world as to when to have the grapes picked. His two sons had graduated from college and were working in high-tech industries in Silicon Valley, so he was on his own until Marta returned.

Riccardo didn't regret much in life. He had a wonderful wife, his children were happy, healthy, and successful, and his vineyard filled his heart and soul. Few men had more, but if he were to regret anything, it would be that the vineyard would not stay in the family when he retired or died. His sons had no interest in it, his wife enjoyed the wine, but had no head for business, and he had not seen any signs of his daughter wanting to take it over, although there were several female vintners in the Sonoma area. Unfortunately, he didn't think Valentina would be one of them.

Ah well, he thought, *it could be much worse. I'm in excellent health and I probably will live for many more years. Who knows? Maybe one of my grandchildren will take over the Neri Winery.*

With that thought cheering him up, he picked up his keys from the hall table and walked out the door. Every time he saw his ATV he smiled. Whoever had designed the all-terrain vehicle must have known how perfect it would be for vintners. They emitted no exhaust smoke, there were no noxious gases of any type due to the fact it was battery-operated, and it was the perfect size to fit between the rows of grapes in his vineyard. It was if the machine had been made for the wine industry.

Riccardo was very predictable and very thorough. Every week he followed a schedule as to which sections of his vineyard he would inspect on a certain day. It was a joke among the vintners, but he was well-liked, so they laughed with him rather than at him. Today was

Tuesday, the day he would go to the far end of his property and check those grapes for their sugar content.

He knew he was one of the few vintners who didn't rely on a refractometer to measure the sugar content of the grapes. The other winemakers constantly talked about the sugar levels they'd detected by taking the sample from the grape and testing it with a refractometer, but he trusted his sense of taste far more than some fancy scientific contraption. For Riccardo, winemaking was an art, not a science. There was no substitute for a well-refined palette, a delicate nose, and a love for the vines and the earth from which they came.

Riccardo turned off his ATV, stepped out of it, and took a moment to breathe in the fresh early morning Northern California air. It was late September and the nights and early mornings were cool in the vineyards. White fluffy clouds gently floated against the brilliant blue sky. He smiled, thinking he must be the luckiest man in the world. Not a day went by when he didn't think something similar.

He walked halfway down a row of grapevines and plucked a grape from one of the vines. *They're almost ready*, he thought. *Better tell Pedro, my vineyard manager, to start hiring in preparation for the crush which will probably take place within the week.*

Riccardo picked another grape and closed his eyes, his total concentration fixed on the taste of the grape in his mouth. When he opened his eyes, he saw a familiar figure approaching him. "Well, look who's here," he said. "I'm surprised to see you clear out here in the vineyard." Those were the last words ever to pass his lips.

A few days after the coroner had completed his investigation, he noted that a crushed grape skin had been found in the decedent's mouth.

CHAPTER THREE

Sam Harris and Guy Jamison met at the main door and walked down the stairs to the room that had the words "HaJam Owners Tasting Room" affixed in large brass letters to its heavy oak door. The room was only used occasionally by Sam and Guy, and it was for a very special purpose. When they were in the room, they would open and share an unreleased bottle of wine that they had produced to determine if it had aged properly and was ready for release to the commercial market.

The HaJam Cellar was known throughout the world for producing superior cabernet sauvignon wines. The grapes in the vineyard had been planted in the early 20th century and many of the bottles they opened had been aged for over ten years.

Guy and Sam had met when they were students in the Viticulture and Enology, better known as winemaking, program at the University of California at Davis, not far from the Napa and Sonoma areas of California. Both of them had been outstanding students, and as the sons of winemakers, they were very interested in having their own winery. While they were in college, they often talked about going into business together, but both of them knew it was probably a pipe dream, given the fact that neither one of them had the money needed to buy a winery.

After graduation they'd each returned to their family's vineyard and worked, but their dream of having their own vineyard remained. Guy thought back to when Sam had called to tell him that one of the oldest vineyards and wineries in Sonoma was on the market. The widow who had inherited it had no children and had tried, with some limited outside help, to keep it going by herself, but without her husband's business and wine knowledge, the property had become rundown, and she couldn't afford the field help that was needed to keep the vineyard productive.

It had been an eyesore for years and wine had finally stopped being made on the property due to the neglected vineyards. When she died, she left everything to her only heir, a great-nephew who lived in New York. He was a hedge fund broker and loved his high-powered lifestyle in Manhattan. He told the lawyer who was handling the estate to sell it to a willing buyer, which to the lawyer meant, "Just unload it real quick and give me the proceeds."

Sam had found out about the pending sale of the property before it had even gone on the market. His father had the flu and had asked Sam to keep an appointment he'd scheduled with his lawyer and go in his place. While Sam was in the lawyer's office, the lawyer received a telephone call and he had to excuse himself in order to take the call. It was a return call from a broker who specialized in wine country real estate.

Sam couldn't help but overhear the conversation and when the lawyer concluded the call, he spoke up. "Excuse me, but I overheard your call, and I'm very interested in the property. Would you give me forty-eight hours to see if I can come up with the money?"

The lawyer agreed. As soon as Sam got in his car he called Guy and told him about the winery going on the market. They spent the next two days talking to everyone they knew who might be able to loan them money. They were able to get the financing by offering favorable terms in return for a flexible payback structure. Sam called the lawyer, the lawyer called the broker, and he and Guy soon became the owners of a winery.

But what to name it? Neither one was married, so wives and

children's names were not possible. Neither one of them was Italian and a lot of the well-known winemakers were, so they didn't want to put their surnames on their labels. In a flash of inspiration Guy said, "What about HaJam, a combination of our last two names? It's short enough that it will fit nicely on the wine bottle labels and interesting enough for people to ask where it comes from?"

"Perfect. Done deal," Sam eagerly responded.

They moved into the house on the property, and although it was quite rundown, it was large. As a realtor would say, "It had great bones." The following year was spent doing back-breaking work, often involving eighteen-hour days.

Having grown up in Sonoma they knew almost all of the vintners––a very tight and supportive group. The vintners offered to help the two young men, however they could, and Sam and Guy took them up on their offers, borrowing equipment and doing anything and everything they could to save money while they got the winery up and running.

Two years later their hard work paid off when they hired a crew of seasonal workers for their first harvest and crush. They bottled the wines, making several different varieties, and then six months later began their first tastings in the HaJam Room. After they had completed several tastings in the HaJam Room, it became well known in the wine community that if they liked the bottle of wine they sampled, then a new release would soon be coming from the HaJam Winery. It was rare that either of them could go anywhere without being asked when they were going down to the HaJam Room. Even the non-wine merchants in town knew about it.

As they did every time they opened a new bottle, they kept to their ritual of carefully wiping clean the special Baccarat crystal wine glasses they'd bought several years earlier and were only used on the evenings they opened a new bottle of wine in the HaJam Room. There was definitely a sense of pomp and ceremony about their tasting ritual. It was serious business and everyone who worked at the winery knew not to bother them on the evenings when they were in the HaJam room.

They lit candles in the room when they entered it and the warm glow of the candles played off of the red brick walls. Sam took the special corkscrew Guy had given him as a present when they'd sold their first case of wine, called a Laguiole En Aubrac corkscrew. It was from France's Laguiole region, famed for its expertly crafted knives. It was the work of a single master cutter whose craft began with shaping the wood handle and concluded with the fitting of the stainless-steel corkscrew implement.

Sam poured them each a small amount of the special cabernet sauvignon they wanted to test, and in true wine tradition, they each picked up their glass, swirled the contents, examined the color, and looked at it to see if it had "legs," or the ability to hold a little of its texture as traces on the sides of the glass made their way back to the wine at the bottom of the glass.

Guy was just getting ready to lift his glass off the table and take a sip when the door to the HaJam Room unexpectedly opened. They both looked up in shock. No one ever dared to open the door. In fact, the only other person who was allowed in the room was the cleaning lady who kept it in perfect condition. When the person opening the door smiled at them, Sam said, "It's nice to see you, but let's talk about whatever you've come for tom…"

Those were the last words Sam ever said. Guy, looking on in dismay, never had a chance to say anything. The killer fired one shot into each of them in rapid order. Without a sound, Sam and Guy fell dead on the floor, each with a single bullet wound to the heart. Interestingly, when the sheriff and his men came the next day, they found the wine just as it had been, resting perfectly in each glass, untouched.

CHAPTER FOUR

Nicola Ferlante, Nick to his friends, and there were many, looked around the tasting room and smiled. It was his favorite time of the day, or evening. The tasting room closed at 7:00 every night, and although he was the owner of the Ferlante Winery, which had been in the family for three generations, three nights a week, Wednesday, Thursday, and Saturday, he poured the wines produced by his vineyard for his customers.

It was rare that a customer ever left the Ferlante tasting room without a case or two of the pinot noir wines for which the boutique winery was famous. And everyone in the Sonoma area agreed that no one could talk a better game about pinot noir, from the color of the grapes to the flavors and aromas that included roses, fruits, black cherry, berry and currant, than Nick himself. He always pointed out the high acidity and low tannins, and assumed everyone in earshot knew exactly what he was talking about.

Even those people who never could figure out what aroma they were smelling or if what they tasted was a tannin, they were simply charmed by the rotund vintner with his hearty laugh, bright blue eyes, and a zest for life.

Nick looked at his watch and at the line forming in front of the cash register where his assistant, Lucia, was happily ringing up sales. She'd worked for him for years and on the nights when he wasn't in the tasting room, Friday and Sunday, she took over. The tasting room was closed to the public on Mondays and Tuesdays.

Usually on Wednesdays, Thursdays, and Saturdays, in addition to the customers, there would be several local Sonoma vintners present in the tasting room. Nick was known not only for his pinot noirs, but also for welcoming his friends when they closed their wineries for the day. The tasting room was warm and inviting, just like Nick.

Sundays Nick tried to stay away from the work of the winery, often not successfully, so he could spend the day with his wife, Anna, and their children, Alessandro and Gabriela. His deepest hope was that his son, Alessandro, would want to work in the Ferrante Winery with him, and maybe even Gabriela. More and more women were working in the wine industry, and several of the local winery owners were women.

Nick had taken over the winery when his father had officially retired, just like his father before him. But the word retirement had little meaning to Paolo and although he said he was retired, he was out in the vineyards at dawn and rarely came back before dusk, because there was no place he would rather be.

The night he didn't return they found him in one of the rows, dead from a heart attack. Paolo and Nick had been very close and Nick still missed him, but he took solace knowing that Paolo had died as he would have wished, swiftly, and in his vineyard.

The learning curve had been high but having grown up in the industry, Nick was able to avoid a lot of the mistakes new vintners often make. The family's roots were deep in the community and the Ferlante family was well thought of. Nick was always more than happy to have his father's friends and fellow vintners give him a little advice. He appreciated it and felt that was one reason the winery had been even more successful than when Paolo had been alive.

Nick had studied wine at the University of California Davis campus and had learned a lot about the newer methods that were being used in modern day wine production. Paolo was of the old school, and whenever Nick had suggested that this or that be changed, his words had fallen on deaf ears.

The last customer of the day walked out after Lucia assured him that the six cases of wine he'd ordered would be shipped to his home the following week. "Lucia, get out of here," Nick said. "You've worked hard enough today. I'll cork the open bottles, and Jenna will be here in the morning to take care of cleaning the wine glasses and wiping down the tables. As usual, thank you. I don't know what I'd do without you."

"Are you sure, Nick? I don't mind staying and helping."

Even as the conversation was taking place, they both knew it was a mere formality, as did everyone else who knew them well. Nick always stayed for at least half an hour after Lucia left. He used that time to think about what needed to be done at the winery, often taking a sip or two from this bottle or that, debating what he could do to make it better.

"Yes, I'm absolutely certain. I'm sure your husband is probably cooking dinner now, waiting for you to walk in the front door. Go, I'll see you tomorrow."

Lucia took off her apron and put it in the pile of dish rags and towels for Jenna to take care of, blew Nick a kiss, and walked out the door in the fading sunlight.

Nick corked the opened bottles and dropped the empty ones in the big recycle trash barrel in the corner. One of Hector's jobs, his full-time handyman, was to come into the tasting room every morning and replace the trash barrel with a fresh one before they opened at eleven. He wiped down the counter, which had spills of pinot noir wine on it, and threw out the contents of the plastic containers where people had poured out the wine they didn't want, common if one wanted to remain sober when wine-tasting.

He always could tell a true wine connoisseur from someone out to have a good time. The connoisseur would order a flight (usually three or five different glasses of wine), take a sip from each, and throw the remaining contents of the glass in the plastic container. The good-time people would order a flight and drink all of the wine in each glass. Nick was always glad to see the hired limousines in his parking lot. He thought drinking wine was a good thing, but driving and drinking wine was a bad thing.

Nick was a good friend of the Dean of Viticulture and Enology at Davis, and the dean hand-picked three students from the university each year to work at the Ferlante Winery as part of their studies. The interns were required to work with Lucia, scheduling time in the tasting room so there were always two people on duty until Nick came in at four on Wednesday, Thursday, and Saturday afternoons.

He picked up one of the bottles of wine that had not been selling well and decided to pour a glass and see if he could figure out why it wasn't selling. He held the glass up to his nose in order to inhale the different aromas. He never had a chance to determine if the wine had a taste of berries or some other elements. The person who opened the door to the tasting room and shot Nick with a single bullet to his heart was very quick and accurate, hitting their target the first time.

Unfortunately, it was Anna, Nick's wife, who discovered his body when he hadn't returned from the tasting room for an unreasonable amount of time. Nick never lived to see if Alessandro would take over the winery.

CHAPTER FIVE

"I could get used to this, Mike. This is my first time in a private plane." Kelly lazed in the butter soft leather of the reclining seat, admiring the walnut trim and plush carpet, unlike anything she had previously seen in an airplane cabin. The engine noise was barely audible, and soothing piped-in music lulled her even further into a state of relaxation. "I'm not sure if I'll ever be able to travel in coach again."

"Enjoy it while you can, Kelly." Mike gave her an affection grin. "Other than when the plane takes us back to Cedar Bay, I don't think there are many more trips on a private jet in our future. And from the way he looks, Rebel seems to be doing just fine on his maiden flight in an airplane."

He looked over at the big boxer who was fast asleep on the dog cushion they'd brought with them. "It was kind of nice not to have to go through security and all that stuff. The only downside was the drive into the private airport in Portland, but I guess that's a small price to pay for this kind of luxury. And spending two hours flying time instead of around eight driving, definitely is a plus."

"Did Sheriff Dawson give you any idea of what we're supposed to do when we get there?"

"Not really. He's picking us up at the airport and taking us directly to the Lugano Winery, where the owner is putting us up. Other than that, I guess we'll just have to sniff out whatever we can. It sounds like a serial killer, but I've never dealt with one, so this is pretty new territory for me."

"Well, if it's new for you, you can imagine what it's like for me." Kelly looked out the window and let out a small gasp. "Mike, you've got to look out your window. It's nothing but miles and miles of vineyards interspersed with houses and big wineries. It's really beautiful."

Mike wriggled around in his seat for a better look. "At least the setting will be nice, and Sheriff Dawson said the accommodations at the winery where we're staying are spectacular. Evidently the owner keeps a guest house there for her best customers. We're just fortunate that none of her best customers were planning on visiting her winery right now. Got your seat belt on? I can see the airport, so we're pretty close."

Kelly smiled. "I'm ready for whatever, just have no idea what whatever will involve."

*****

When they walked down the stairway of the plane, a man was waiting for them at the bottom of the stairs. Easily over 6'2" with salt and pepper hair and a developing paunch, he carried himself with such an air of authority that people who didn't know him were usually quite intimidated, which was fine with him. Being the sheriff in a tourist destination area that catered to wealthy wine connoisseurs, he'd met more than his share of people who thought their money could get them out of a ticket after a little too much wine-tasting. They were wrong.

"Mike, Kelly, it's good to see you again." Sheriff Ted Dawson greeted them with a handshake before bending down and scratching Rebel behind his ears. "I'm glad you brought your dog." He regarded Kelly with a smile. "I believe when I first met Mike he told me you had a guard dog who was usually with you when you were involved in helping Mike solve a case. I'm not sure what this big guy can do, but if he's helped in the past, I could sure use his help now."

Straightening up, Ted continued, "I really appreciate you two coming down here and helping me out. I know I ruined your vacation, but the good news is that you'll be staying in the lap of luxury at Julie's guest house. And Kelly, I remembered that you owned a restaurant, so I took the liberty of calling a couple of my friends who own restaurants in Sonoma and making dinner reservations for you for tonight and tomorrow night."

He turned and introduced them to the young deputy who was standing next to a black and white sheriff's car. "This is my deputy, Josh Matthews. I wanted you to meet him. If there's something you need and I'm not available, he's the one to call." Josh opened the rear door of the patrol car for Mike, Kelly, and Rebel, and a few minutes later, they pulled into the sheriff station parking lot.

"I've set up a meeting in my office so you can meet Kevin O'Reilly who is my lead investigator in these murder cases." He nodded to his receptionist as the three of them, along with Rebel, walked down the hall.

Ted opened the door to his office and introduced them to a man who appeared to be in his late 30's. He looked like he worked out regularly and had a thick black mustache, wore his hair short, and had a dark complexion. Vivid green eyes with the dark complexion made Kelly think he was what her mother used to call Black Irish.

"Mike, Kelly, this is Detective Kevin O'Reilly. He's the lead detective on the case we're calling The Wine Country Killer, for obvious reason." They shook hands and then Sheriff Dawson indicated for everyone to take a seat.

"Excuse me, Rebel," Sheriff Dawson said. "I didn't mean to ignore you.Kevin, this is Rebel, and from what I understand, one of the best murder-solving dogs in Oregon."

Kevin leaned over and held his hand out for Rebel to sniff. Rebel sniffed it, then backed up, and stood next to Kelly and Mike.

"Don't take it personally, Kevin," Kelly said. "Sometimes it takes Rebel a little time to warm up to people."

"No problem. Trust me, in this line of work a lot of people don't warm up to me." He stepped back and sat down.

"Kevin, why don't you fill Mike and Kelly in about the four murders that have occurred. Mike, I had one of my clerks photocopy the file and you can take it with you. If Kevin told you everything about the case, we'd be here all day and night."

CHAPTER SIX

Kevin cleared his throat and began to speak. "Let's start with the first murder which occurred six months ago, just before the crush. The victim was Riccardo Neri, and he was murdered in his vineyard by a single gunshot to his heart. A man of few words, he was well regarded in both the industry and the community alike.

"We've found no indication that he had problems with his employees or anyone else. Actually, that's a recurring theme in all of these murders. All of the victims were well-liked, and we've never even developed a viable suspect in any of the them. His winery was known for the chardonnay wines they produced.

"Excuse me, Kevin," Mike said, "did any of the victims have ex-spouses or family problems?"

Kevin shook his head. "No, none. The next killing occurred at the HaJam Winery. The owners, Sam Harris and Guy Jamison were murdered while they were in a small private tasting room in their winery next to where the barrels were aged. They had a ritual every month or so of opening a bottle of wine in the HaJam Room at the winery to see if it was ready for release.

"They usually talked about when they were going to have one of their tastings in the HaJam Room, so it was no secret where they'd be. The killer used the same method to kill both of them that was used in the Meri murder, namely a single gunshot to the heart. And again, no suspects." He glanced down at his file before continuing.

"The HaJam Winery is known for its excellent cabernet sauvignon wines. The two victims were unmarried and lived in the house attached to the winery. We've found no evidence of any kind of personal or business scandal involving either of them. We found no evidence of lovers or disgruntled exes. They'd grown up in Sonoma, as had all the victims, and were extremely well thought of. They were murdered three months ago.

"Last, but not least, the most recent murder occurred two weeks ago. Nick, actually his name is Nicola Ferlante, was murdered in the tasting room of his winery. He was a third generation Sonoma vintner and again, popular with everyone we spoke to. He, too was killed by a single gunshot."

"Excuse me, Kevin," Kelly said. "This is probably a dumb question, but I'm assuming that the same gun was used in the four killings."

"No, that's not a dumb question and yes, it was the same gun as verified by ballistic tests. Back to Nick. His tasting room was a popular place for a lot of the vintners to go when they ended their day, so on almost any given evening when Nick was there on Wednesdays, Thursdays, or Saturdays, there would be a few vintners from the nearby area present.

"He followed pretty much the same schedule on the evenings he worked in the tasting room. He would tell his help to go home, stay for a while in the tasting room, I assume thinking about his pinot noir wines, and then lock up and head for home. Unfortunately, the night of the murder he never went home. His wife was the one who discovered his body." Kevin looked around the group, his mouth knit in a tight line.

Mike had been taking notes the whole time Kevin had been talking. "Kevin, there seem to be some similarities here. All of the vintners were well-known in the area, produced very good wines, and none of them seemed to be involved in any type of scandal. What else occurs to me is that it looks like the murderer, actually we could probably call him or her a serial killer, is stepping up the pace of the murders. How is this affecting the other vintners in the area?"

"I can answer that, Mike," Sheriff Dawson said. "I'm good friends with a lot of them. I grew up here and have known all of them forever. They're a tight group and contrary to what people would think, since they're in the same industry, they really support one another. In a nutshell, they're scared to death, and that's one of the reasons I asked you and Kelly to come help me out.

"They held a meeting a few days ago, and unbeknownst to me, they all put up quite a bit of money to hire someone to help catch the killer. They think maybe the killer is someone known to them and possibly from around this area. They think it's odd that the killer seemed to know the patterns or the habits of each of the men murdered. I called you before they told me about the fund, but it will go to pay for your expenses. I could have covered your costs, but it really would have stretched my department's budget."

"And I assume that's why we were picked up in Portland and are staying at a very nice winery. Is that correct, Sheriff?" Kelly asked.

"Yes. They thought it would be good to have a fresh set of eyes look at this case. They made it very apparent they don't think my department has mishandled the case in any way, but I guess it's kind of like going to a doctor for a second opinion. Sometimes it helps."

"We'll certainly do what we can," Mike said. "I'd like to study the file tonight and get a sense of what we're dealing with. Kevin, I appreciate the information you've given us. I think Kelly and I will head for the winery where we're staying, get settled, have dinner, and I'll start my investigation after dinner. Okay with you?"

"That's fine, Mike." Sheriff Dawson pushed a piece of paper across the desk. "Kelly, here's the information on the two restaurants where I made reservations for you. They're in my name, since the owners are both good friends of mine. There's an unmarked car out in the parking lot that I've arranged for you to use while you're here in Sonoma. I've also written down the directions to the Lugano winery where you'll be staying. It's really something, and I'll be curious what you think of the guest house. Quite frankly, it's about as large as the house I live in."

Kelly accepted the information, and the sheriff stood up. "Let's plan on getting together tomorrow afternoon after you've had a chance to read the file and tried to absorb everything," he said, walking around his desk and showing them to the door. "Give me a call when you're ready and Kelly, Mike, thanks again for coming. And you too, Rebel."

CHAPTER SEVEN

"Mike, I know we're here because murders have taken place, but even so, I still think this is one of the most beautiful places I've ever been." Kelly was awestruck by the scenery on the way to the guest house. "It's almost like it's out of some fairy tale murder. Rolling hills covered with vineyards interrupted sporadically by incredible wineries. It's certainly something we don't see in sleepy little Cedar Bay. I can't wait to see the Lugano Winery."

"I think when you see where we're staying, you're going to be amazed." Mike, who was driving, gave her a sideways glance. "I looked it up on the internet after I called Sheriff Dawson back to tell him we were coming. If it lives up to the internet experience, we can pretend we're on vacation, rather than investigating murders."

"After the meeting we just had, that would be a relief. Dealing with a serial killer is a first for me. It seems to go beyond the normal passions that led to the other murders I've helped you with."

"Agreed. Look Kelly, over there on the hill to the left. That's the Lugano Winery, where we'll be staying. The information the chief gave us said to drive around to the back and go to the larger house where Julie Lugano lives. He said the other house we'll see is where we'll be staying."

Mike put his indicator on and turned up a small road that led to the winery. The parking lot in front of the winery was filled with cars and limousines.

"Mike, that may be the most spectacular building I've ever seen. With the green ivy covering the imposing stone front and the perfectly trimmed privets surrounding the building, it is absolutely beautiful. It looks like an old castle, kind of like the ones we saw when we were in Italy at the cooking school. It's even grander than the one we stayed in while we were there. What's just as impressive is the backdrop. I mean look at those rugged mountains. And the never-ending hill after rolling hill of grapevines. It's like stepping into a painting in real life."

Mike drove through the parking lot, past the front of the castle, and then followed a narrow driveway that looped around behind it. Attached to the rear of the castle was a large stone house, with a smaller freestanding replica next to it, both covered with ivy, emulating the castle.

He parked in front of the house and said, "I think it would be wise for us to leave Rebel in the car until we get a lay of the land. Don't want him scaring our hostess."

"That was really thoughtful of Sheriff Dawson to get that fold-up kennel for Rebel and put it in the trunk," Kelly said as they climbed out of the car. "Even though he assured us that he'd cleared having Rebel stay with us in the guest house, it made me feel better. He's used to his at home, so I know he'll be fine with it."

"Agreed. Let's go, Kelly. Time to meet the owner of the Lugano Winery, Julie Lugano." They followed the winding stone walkway up to the house and rang the doorbell. A few moments later the door was opened by a beautiful Italian looking young woman with jet-black shoulder-length hair, a dark complexion, and the largest deep brown eyes Kelly had ever seen.

"May I help you?" the young woman asked.

"Yes," Mike said. "I'm Sheriff Mike Reynolds, and this is my wife

Kelly. Sheriff Dawson made arrangements with Julie Lugano for us to stay in the guest house for a few days."

"Of course, Sheriff. Julie told me she was expecting you. I'm Alessia, Julie's niece. Please come in. I'll go get Julie."

A few moments later a woman who appeared to be in her 50's walked down the hall and into the large living room where Alessia had taken Mike and Kelly. She walked over to them and held out her lily-white hand. "Welcome to the Lugano Winery. I'm Julie Lugano. Ted told me you were coming, and I volunteered for you to stay in my guest house. Follow me and I'll take you there."

She turned and said, "Alessia, if Ted calls, please tell him that the sheriff and his wife have arrived safely, and I'm getting them settled in the guest house. Tell him I'll see him tonight at the winery owners' meeting." She turned back to Mike and Kelly and said, "Please, this way." She opened the heavy door and they followed her to the guest accommodation located next to the main house.

*****

All three of them, Julie, Kelly, and Mike, walked over to the sprawling guest house that had been built in the same style as the winery, a Tuscan style one-story building with a red door matching the one at Julie's home. Julie opened it and said, "Here we are. It has a full kitchen, and I had Alessia stock the refrigerator.

"Ted told me he'd arranged for you to have dinner at restaurants tonight and tomorrow night, but there's plenty of food in there for breakfast and lunch. I also took the liberty of having Alessia put a couple of bottles of our wines in the kitchen. I believe the whites are in the refrigerator. Please help yourself, I'll show you the bedrooms," she said as she walked down the hall.

Kelly was quiet while she followed Julie, then she said, "Julie, I think this is larger than our home in Cedar Bay. It's absolutely beautiful. The furnishings and the decorative touches are lovely. Did you do it yourself or have it done?"

"Thanks, Kelly. I did all of it myself. I was an interior decorator when I met Mario. After we were married I did a little bit of it, but he really wanted me to help him run the winery." A bittersweet smile crossed her face. "It's been in his family for several generations and is well known throughout the world for its fine wines. As it turned out it was a blessing, because when he died unexpectedly, I became the one in charge. We have no children and Mario was an only child. His parents are deceased, and there really is no one else."

"That must have been very difficult for you, even though you'd been running it with him," Mike said.

"Yes, but I was just as concerned about what would happen to it when I'm gone. You met Alessia. I call her my niece, but she's actually she's more of a shirt-tail niece through Mario's cousins who still live in Italy. I didn't want the winery to pass out of the Lugano family, so I wrote to a cousin of his I'd never met and asked him if he had a family member who would like to come to the United States and learn about how we make wine. The family still has a winery in Italy."

"How wise of you," Kelly said. "How long has Alessia been with you and is it working out?"

Julie's blue eyes sparkled. "Mario's been gone for five years, and she came here a few months after he died. And yes, it's working out beautifully. In fact, I depend more and more on her every day. I'm comfortable now knowing that if something should happen to me the winery would not only stay in the Lugano family, it would be run by a very competent person."

"Well, judging by how healthy you look, it seems that's going to be quite far off in the future," Kelly said.

Later, she'd remember those words and realize how wrong she'd been.

CHAPTER EIGHT

"Okay, Kelly, I've set up Rebel's kennel, put his soft bed in it, and fed him. You've unpacked for us. Anything else we need to do before we go out to dinner? It's been a long day, and I'm getting hungry." Mike rubbed his stomach. "What time are the dinner reservations?"

"They're for seven, and I think we better leave considering we're not exactly sure where the restaurant is located. I'll put Rebel in his kennel while you make sure everything's locked up."

"Mission accomplished, Kelly. Do you have the restaurant information?"

"I do. It's in my purse, and I even did a search on the internet, and I know exactly were it is. Remember where the town square is? Well, it's just off of it about a half block."

Fifteen minutes later they walked into a small Italian restaurant and gave Sheriff Dawson's name to the hostess. A moment later a big burly Italian man walked out of the kitchen and said, "Sheriff Reynolds, welcome to Giovanni's. And welcome to you, Mrs. Reynolds. I'm Giovanni, the owner of this fine establishment. Ted called and said you'd be coming. Please, follow me."

He led them through the crowded dining room to a corner table adorned with a pristine tablecloth and a flickering candle. "I hope this is satisfactory. Ted also insisted that I present you with a bottle of Sonoma wine from one of the best wineries in the area, a pinot noir from the Ferrante Vineyard. He didn't know what you'd be eating, but a good pinot noir goes with about everything. *Buon appetito!*"

"Thank you. We've definitely been looking forward to this."

"Let me pour your wine," he said taking a corkscrew out of his back pocket and deftly opening the bottle. "I'll be back later. Your server will be Battista," he said as he hurried back to the kitchen, delayed by customers' handshakes and kisses. Judging from the completely full dining room, it was obvious Giovanni's and its owner were very popular.

"Mike, we must thank Ted when we see him tomorrow," Kelly said, taking in her surroundings. "This restaurant is every bit as lovely as what we saw in Italy. In fact, it looks like a replica, from the starched white linens to the candles everywhere you look. Murder, or I should say, murders, is nothing to celebrate, but I think we're going to eat well while we're here."

"Try a sip of your wine. I know we're not connoisseurs, but given that Ted asked for us to have it, and it's from a winery owned by one of the victims, I would think it's pretty good."

They'd each just taken a sip of their wine when a handsome young Italian man walked up to their table and handed them menus. "*Buonasera,*" he said with a smile that deepened the dimples on his cheeks. "My name is Battista, and I will be your server this evening.

"Giovanni wanted me to tell you that we do have one of his favorites this evening, a salmon pasta with a creamy garlic sauce. A friend of his just returned from Legacy Lodge in British Columbia with over forty pounds of salmon filets, and he gave Giovanni half of it. The salmon is flash frozen, so it has a very fresh taste. The only time Giovanni prepares this dish is when his friend returns from Canada. It's the only salmon served here at the restaurant, because Giovanni feels no salmon he can source is as good as the salmon from Legacy Lodge.

"I might suggest our house special Italian salad to go along with it and some garlic bread. The salad is fresh romaine and iceberg lettuce from Giovanni's garden with cherry tomatoes, pepperoncini, red onion, and black olives with a classic Italian dressing. I'll tell you about the desserts after you've finished your main course, because I don't want to confuse you."

"Sold," Kelly said, snapping her menu shut and handing it to him.

"That makes two of us. If the owner suggests something, who am I to ignore the message?" Mike said with a laugh.

Battista responded with a nod and a smile. "Your salads will be here in a few minutes."

Kelly looked after him and said, "If I had a second daughter and she was unmarried, I think I know where I'd bring her to dinner."

"Well, it's probably a good thing you don't. For all you know Battista may be happily married. With dimples like that, I hope so for his wife's sake."

The salmon and salad were excellent, and they both agreed that trying to cook the salmon at home or at Kelly's Koffee Shop would be a waste of time and money. The freshness of the salmon was what made it so good, but Kelly was determined to try and duplicate the salad when she got home. It shouldn't be that hard. As she often did when they went out to dinner, she took out the small notebook she kept in her purse and wrote down exactly what was in the salad. The dressing she wasn't too worried about.

"Mike, I think I'll pass on dessert. I ate far more bread than I should have and obviously, since there's nothing left of either the salmon pasta or the salad, I ate all of that as well. Quite frankly, I'm stuffed."

"Agreed." He looked over to where Battista was standing and nodded.

"I see you enjoyed my suggestions. That will make Giovanni happy. For dessert…"

Mike held up his hand. "Battista, thank you, but no thanks. We're done. The only thing we need is the check."

"I wish I could help you with that, sir, but your dinner has been taken care of, compliments of Sheriff Dawson. I'm sure Giovanni will tell him how much you enjoyed it. And Giovanni asked me to tell you that he's sorry he couldn't make it back to your table, but as you can see, we're quite busy tonight."

"Tell him I understand completely. Thank you, and I'll thank Ted myself when I see him tomorrow," Mike said as he and Kelly both stood up. As they walked to their car, he said, "Kelly, I need to get back to the house and read the file. It might take a little while, so feel free to go to bed without me."

When they got back to the guest house, Mike kissed Kelly good night and went into the study with his briefcase and the file. Kelly took Rebel out for a walk, got ready for bed, picked up her iPad to finish the book she'd been reading on the plane, and was fast asleep before she finished the first page.

CHAPTER NINE

Kelly felt a warm muzzle on her cheek and opened her eyes. Rebel was standing next to her, and she recognized the look on his face and in his eyes. She carefully swung her legs over the edge of the bed, trying not to wake Mike up, but she was unsuccessful.

"Morning, love," he said groggily. "What time is it?"

"According to the clock on the nightstand, it's 7:00 a.m. What time did you come to bed last night?" she asked as she secured the tie on her robe, preparing to walk Rebel before feeding him his breakfast.

"I think it was around midnight," Mike said with a yawn. "You fell asleep with the light on. Feel rested?"

"Yes, probably a lot more so than you do. Learn anything last night?"

"Just the specifics, but the facts were pretty much what Kevin and Ted told us." He pulled himself up into a sitting position. "They were all high-end winery owners and male. No signs of a struggle, but the alarming thing is that the serial killer, if we can call him that, and I think we can, is lessening the time between his kills, frighteningly so. I can see why the wine owners are nervous. I'll be curious what Julie has to say about the Winery Owners Association meeting she went to last night."

"She mentioned that whenever someone stayed in the guest house, even though there are breakfast makings here, she thinks it's nicer if the guests eat breakfast with her," Kelly said. "She told me there would be fresh juice and breakfast casseroles. She has a chef who prepares small plates for the people who are sampling wine in the tasting room, and the chef loves to try out new dishes. She said not to expect normal breakfast fare, but it's always good.

The chef has one of her staff deliver the breakfast items to Julie the afternoon before so all Julie has to do is just pop them in the oven the next morning. Julie said it's kind of a win-win situation because she and her guests have wonderful food, and the chef gets to try out new dishes to serve in the tasting room."

"Did she mention a time?" Mike asked as he walked into the bathroom and started the shower.

"Yes, she said 8:00 was a civilized time for breakfast in the wine country. She mentioned that she meditates from 6:30 to 7:30 every morning in the vineyard. She laughed and said she'd started doing it when she was in college, and it's a habit she's never gotten rid of."

"From what I've read, I think that's a good habit to have," Mike said, as steam began to fill the bathroom. "I imagine running a winery this large has to be stressful at times. Think about it. She's got the vineyard, making the wine, marketing the wine, the tasting room, hiring all kinds of people, the bookkeeping, and who knows what else."

"I'm sure she outsources a lot of that, but even so, she's ultimately responsible for it. I'm going to take Rebel out for a walk. We'll be back in a couple of minutes. I'll shower when you're finished."

"With the size of this shower, and all those jets, we could save a lot of time and shower together," Mike said with a lewd grin on his face. "Plus think of all the water we'd save."

"Fraid not, Sheriff, we're here to see if we can help solve a few murders. I just hope no more occur while we're here."

"Don't think that's a problem. There's usually a little time between the murders," he said as he stepped into the shower and began to sing.

*****

"I'm starving, which should be impossible considering the humongous amount of food I ate last night. Maybe I have some metabolic problem," Kelly said as they walked over to Julie's house.

"I think rather than a metabolic problem it's called love of good food, pure and simple," Mike answered as he rang the doorbell.

Thinking that maybe Julie was taking a shower or changing her clothes after her morning meditation, when there was no response, he rang the bell again. A moment later Alessia answered it with a drawn look on her face. "Please, come in."

They entered the hallway and Kelly said, "Alessia you look worried. Is something wrong?"

The young woman frowned. "I'm sure it's nothing, but I can't find Julie anywhere. She's always in the kitchen at this time when we have guests. I know it sounds silly, but with all the murders that have taken place lately…" her voice trailed off as they followed her into the kitchen. Julie wasn't there.

"Did she mention she had an early morning meeting or anything like that?" Mike asked.

"No, and that's something she was always careful to do. She was in the habit of telling me whenever there was a change in her routine, particularly now what with all these murders, because she didn't want me to worry. I hope she's alright," Alessia said as she raised a hand to her mouth and began to chew on one of her thumbnails.

"Alessia, do you know where she meditates?"

"Yes, me and everyone else in Sonoma knows where she goes," she said with a laugh. "Julie is a bit of a creature of habit and never deviates from her morning routine. She always meditates at the foot of a big blue oak tree on the ridge over there." She walked across the kitchen and pointed out the window.

"You can see it from here. She told me Mario's family thought it was a good luck tree because it had always been there and they had prospered from the vineyard. The family felt their luck would change if they removed it, and the tree does seem to thrive there. I read up on it because I'd never heard of an oak tree in a vineyard, but evidently this particular species likes a hot and rocky location and that ridge gets more sun than the rest of the vineyard and it's very rocky."

"Let's take a walk over there. Maybe Julie tripped and fell or something," Mike said. "You know where it is. Lead the way. Kelly, do you want to come with us or stay here in case she returns from somewhere else?"

"No. I'll go with you. Alessia, may I have a piece of paper and a pen? I'll leave her a note that we'll be back in a few minutes."

But Julie wasn't returning.

CHAPTER TEN

Alessia, Mike, and Kelly walked through the vineyard and began to climb up the long sloping ridge. Alessia was pointing out some of the other vineyards that could be seen from that vantage point when Kelly saw something that caused her to cry out. "Oh no." She began running to the oak tree, quickly followed by Alessia and Mike.

They got there too late. Julie was sitting with her back against the tree, a bullet hole through her heart. Alessia dropped to the ground, sobbing and screaming, "No, no, no. Julie, please no." Mike gently put his arm around her and led her a few feet away, knowing that the entire area should now be treated as the scene of a crime. What kept running through Mike's mind were the words *The Wine Country Killer has killed again.*

Kelly sat next to where Alessia had slumped to the ground, her arm around her while the young woman sobbed uncontrollably. Mike said, "Stay here. I need to call Ted and tell him what happened."

Alessia cried out, "Oh, that poor man. He was so in love with Julie. He was going to retire soon, and they were going to get married next year. He was going to help her run the winery."

Mike looked over at Kelly with a shocked expression. "Alessia, I didn't know. Now I see why she hosted us, and she called him Ted. I am so sorry, but I have to make this call."

He stepped several feet away, not wanting Alessia to hear his conversation. Mike took a deep breath and pressed in the numbers for Sheriff Dawson's cell phone.

"Dawson here. Is that you, Mike?" He sounded upbeat.

"Yes, and Ted, I have some very bad news. It looks like The Wine Country Killer has taken another wine owner's life…"

"Mike, please tell me it's not Julie. She's the only one you'd be seeing this early. Please, not her," he said as his voice broke.

Telling Ted that the woman he loved was the woman who had been killed by the serial killer was one of the hardest things Mike had ever done.

After a short pause, Ted spoke. He sounded like a different person to the one who had answered the phone mere seconds earlier. "I'll call Kevin and several of my deputies, and we'll be there in a few minutes."

"Ted, we're on the ridge by the big oak tree."

"I know where it is. Julie went there every morning to meditate, even when I stayed over. How is Alessia?"

"Inconsolable," Mike said ending the call. He walked back to Kelly and Alessia and said, "He'll be here in a few minutes."

"How did he take it?" Kelly asked.

"Professionally, even though I'm sure he's in a complete state of shock. He's having the guy we met yesterday, Kevin, the lead investigator, come as well as several of his deputies. We'll stay here. There's no point in going back to the house."

A few minutes later they heard the sound of sirens and car doors being slammed. Sheriff Dawson scrambled up the ridge and stopped, looking at Julie. "I can't even hug her one more time," he said as he fell to his knees and began sobbing, head bowed.

Alessia stood up and walked over to him, wrapping him in an embrace. "Ted, I am so, so sorry. I can't believe this has happened."

"She was so happy last night." Ted choked back a sob. "We even set the date for our wedding. I gave her the ring she's wearing. This is like a nightmare, and I can't wake up. Seeing my other friends murdered was bad enough, but this, this is the end of my life as well as hers."

By that time several of the sheriff's deputes and Kevin had arrived at the scene. They all looked at the sheriff, not knowing quite what to do. Mike saw that Ted was in no condition to give his men orders, so he took charge.

"I'm Sheriff Mike Reynolds and Sheriff Dawson asked me to come here to see if I could help find this serial killer. I'll be taking his place for the next couple of days." He turned to Sheriff Dawson who had tears running down his cheeks. "Ted, okay with you if I take your place for a little while?"

At this point, the sheriff was too distressed to even talk. Numbly he shook his head, indicating yes. "This is a crime scene," Mike said, taking command. "Treat it as one. I want the winery and the vineyard secured. I want to know where every worker the winery and the vineyard employ was at the time of the murder."

He turned to Alessia and said, "I'm sorry, but I'm going to need your help. I assume you have a vineyard manager as well as a manager for the tasting room. I want them called, and I want them to come to the guest house in one hour."

Mike looked at Kevin and said, "I know you're going to want to talk to them as part of the investigation. We might as well do it together to save time."

"I'll be there in an hour," Keven responded. "I need to see if there are any clues here at the scene. I'll call the coroner." He looked at one of the deputies. "Joe, take the sheriff home and stay with him for a little while. There's really nothing he can do here. Mike, why don't you take Alessia back to the house."

"That's fine." Mike walked over to where Kelly and Alessia were sitting on the ground and gave Alessia his hand, helping her up. Kelly stood up with her and they each put an arm around the young woman, supporting her as they walked down the ridge and through the rows of grapevines to the main house.

CHAPTER ELEVEN

When Kelly, Mike, and Alessia got back to Julie's house, Alessia called José Martinez, the vineyard manager, Ginger Nichols, the woman in charge of the tasting room, and Pete Jennings, the head of security for the vineyard, and arranged for them all to meet with Kevin and Mike at the guest house at 9:30 that morning.

"Why don't you lie down and rest for a little while?" Kelly said to Alessia.

"No, I want to sit in on the meeting," Alessia said. "Julie was like a mother to me, and I want Mike and Kevin to find whoever did this. I need to call Julie's attorney and tell him as well. A winery doesn't have the luxury of taking a few days off. Quite simply things need to be done, things that Julie used to do. She told me that she set up a trust, and that I would inherit everything, but I need to make sure I'm acting in accordance with her wishes and have the authority to do so before I start taking over."

"I think that's a good idea." Kelly thought for a second and then said, "Since the murder took place at quite a distance from the winery, I don't think they'll feel that the winery needs to be closed, but you better ask them. I'd imagine the workers would still be able to work in the vineyards, but just not near the crime scene. You better ask Mike and Kevin about that before you make any decisions. I'll get your phone for you so you can call the attorney. Where is it?"

"It's on the counter in the kitchen. You know, Julie told me several times that she wanted me to take over the winery if anything ever happened to her, and I knew she was grooming me to do that. I just never expected it to be so soon. I hope I learned enough to run it properly, like Julie did."

"From what I've heard, the winery owners in Sonoma are very close to one another. I'm sure there are a number of them who would be happy to help you when you have questions."

"It would be nice if some of them are still alive when I have questions," Alessia said darkly. Kelly didn't know what to say in response to such a chilling scenario, so she simply turned away and went into the kitchen to retrieve Alessia's cell phone.

When she returned with the phone, Alessia called Julie's attorney and told him what had happened. He was devastated and said that Julie had been one of his favorite clients. He told Alessia he'd come by that afternoon to discuss the terms of the trust, but confirmed since she was inheriting the winery, she was free to make any decisions she thought were necessary.

A short time later, Kelly and Alessia walked over to the guest house. Kelly was surprised to see Sheriff Dawson's car parked out in front of it. When they were inside Alessia introduced Kelly and Rebel to José, Ginger, and Pete. Kelly glanced at Ted who looked like he'd aged twenty years since she'd seen him just a little over an hour ago.

"Please everyone, be seated. I know you're all busy, so I'll try to keep this as short as possible. However, the main reason you're here is to find out what you know, if anything, about Julie Lugano's murder. Sheriff Dawson will be taking a leave of absence from his position for a little while, but he wanted to sit in on this meeting. Kevin, this is your investigation, please start," Mike said.

"We're all aware that this is the fifth murder of a wine owner in the Sonoma area within the last few months," Kevin began. "We're pretty sure we're dealing with a serial killer, and we've started calling that person The Wine Country Killer. So saying, we're not any closer to finding out who that person is. Several sheriff's deputies are combing the area around the scene of the crime as we speak. Naturally, we're hoping to find something, but based on the other murders, I'm not overly hopeful. Before we begin, do any of you have questions for me?"

"Yes," Alessia said. "I've confirmed with Julie's attorney what she had always told me, that I'm the beneficiary of the winery, is correct. He told me I have complete authority to do whatever I think needs to be done. Since a crime was committed on the property, will the winery have to be closed while you're investigating the murder?"

"No. The crime was committed far enough away from the winery itself that it won't be necessary to close it. I've instructed my men to secure the immediate crime scene area with yellow police tape, but I've asked them to put it low to the ground. The tasting room doesn't look out on that part of the property, but if someone should see yellow up on the ridge, I think they'll just assume someone thought it was a good place to plant some flowers. It should only be up for a day or so, so you can conduct business as usual."

"Thank you. Will you need to do anything in the wine tasting room? It opens in a few hours, so if you do need something to be done there, I'd like that to be as soon as possible."

"Alessia, that depends on what Ginger has to say." He turned and faced Ginger. "Can you think of anything that took place there in the last couple of days that seemed the least bit suspicious to you? Did any of the help who work in the wine tasting room report anything unusual to you?"

Ginger was quiet for several moments and then said, "When Alessia called me earlier this morning with this horrible news, I tried to reconstruct the last couple of days in my head. I have a pretty good memory and once I've seen a customer, I'll usually remember when that customer returns.

"I've personally been there the last three days while the tasting room was open, because I was training a new person, but in answer to your question, no. The people who were there were either legitimate wine connoisseurs or people out to have a good time. There were no suspicious customers and no indication that the visitors to the tasting room had anything to do with Julie's murder."

"Ginger," Mike said. "You mentioned that you were training someone. Was this someone you knew or simply a new employee?"

She looked at him earnestly. "Sheriff, I've known Mike Craven since he was a little boy. He's my best friend's son. He's graduating from Davis next year with a wine degree, and I told him when he started at Davis that he could work at the winery between his junior and senior year. I would vouch for him with my life."

"That's what I wanted to know, Ginger, thanks."

"José, what about the vineyard workers? Any new hires? Any problems?" Kevin asked.

"No, sir. Miss Julie paid a little more than the other vineyard owners, and I've had the same crew working here for at least three years, maybe longer. They all know each other well. In fact, most of them are related to me, and I can vouch for all of them."

"Thanks. Pete, what about you and your staff?"

"Like Ginger, I've been going over and over this. I find it interesting that the murder took place when Lou, the guard who has the 3:00 a.m. to 11:00 a.m. shift, was taking his usual thirty-minute break at 6:30 this morning. That's about the time the murder took place.

"Security personnel by law are entitled to a work break of at least thirty minutes during their shifts. I suggested several times to Miss Julie that we bring in another guard during break times so we'd be covered, but she thought that was a waste of money. Plus, it would be very difficult to hire responsible security personnel who were willing to work for only half an hour."

"Pete, what does the shift of a security guard here look like?" Mike asked.

"When the winery is open to the public, his main job is just to have his presence known to prevent drunken behavior, fights, things of that nature. When the winery is closed, he patrols the winery and adjacent buildings."

"What about the vineyards? Does he patrol the vineyards?" Mike asked.

"No. Miss Julie felt the winery and building were what was most important from a security aspect. She wasn't too concerned about the vineyards. There has never been an incident here before, and she always said there was no reason to think there would be now."

"Even with the murders that have taken place," Mike said.

Pete raised an eyebrow. "Yes. We talked about that. Everyone has a theory about the murders, and Julie thought they were being committed by someone who had known the victims. She didn't think she knew anyone capable of murder, so even when I suggested we hire more security, she said no." His expression faltered. "Now I wish I would have insisted."

"Ginger, José, Pete, I think you can leave," Kevin said. "I don't have any more questions, do you Mike?"

"No, thank you for taking the time to come, and if you think of anything, I'm staying here at the guest house, so please feel free to come see me."

CHAPTER TWELVE

After the winery employees had left the guest house, Mike turned to Ted. "Ted, I'm sorry to do this, but I believe you saw Julie last night at the Winery Owner's Association meeting. Did she seem anxious or nervous? In other words, I guess what I'm asking is if you know whether or not she'd been threatened or anything like that."

Sheriff Dawson was quiet for several moments before he replied. "Yes, I was with her last night at the meeting. It was held at a restaurant in town. We used to meet at different wineries, but after this last murder, that is, the murder before Julie..." Ted choked up and had to stop talking. He took a moment to try and compose himself while a single teardrop trickled down his cheek.

Finally, Ted continued, "The winery owners, as you can well imagine, have become very skittish because of the murders. As a matter of fact," he said looking at Rebel, "several of them have gotten dogs who are with them at all times. Our department has done business with a dog trainer who specializes in guard dogs and some of the owners have bought four or five of them from him.

"In full disclosure, I have to tell you that the dog trainer is my nephew. Anyway, I'd asked Julie several times to get one, but she always laughed it off." He put his head in his hands, and everyone in the room was quiet for several moments, silently respecting the agony and grief Ted was going through.

He looked up and resumed. "Julie felt because she was a woman she was safe. She thought whoever it was only targeted men. Obviously, she was wrong, and it cost her life."

Kevin said, "Sorry, Ted, but to get back to what Mike asked. Did you have any sense that she felt she was in danger? Was she nervous or anxious?"

"Not in the least." Ted let out a hollow sigh. "As I said, she didn't feel female winery owners were targets, and she even said that at the meeting. She was telling everyone how glad she was that I had called Mike, and he had agreed to come to Sonoma and see what he could find out. She said she felt very safe having him here, particularly since he'd be staying next door in her guest house."

"Well, I guess I certainly failed her there," Mike said with a stricken look on his face.

"No, Mike, Julie would have really been angry if you'd tried to watch over her or do anything special." Ted was emphatic. "She was very strong in her views, and her view was that she was safe here at her winery. Believe me, whatever you might have said to her would have fallen on deaf ears."

"I wish I'd said something," Kelly said, and everyone turned to her. "The thought occurred to me last night that living in that big house and with the murders that had taken place, maybe I should have asked her if she'd like Rebel to stay with her."

She looked towards Alessia and said, "Since I didn't do that, I think you should take Rebel while we're here and keep him close to you. After all, you're now a winery owner and could possibly be on the killer's hit list. Rebel's well-trained, and I can practically guarantee you that nothing will happen to you with him here."

"Thanks, Kelly. I appreciate the offer, but as you can see from my red eyes and my runny nose, I'm extremely allergic to dogs. I'm sure you all thought I look the way I do because of Aunt Julie's murder, and of course there is that. But most of it is because of Rebel." She gazed across at Rebel with sad eyes. "Sorry, big guy. That's just the way it is."

"I wish you would have told me, and I would have put him in another room. As a matter of fact, I'll do that right now," Kelly said, feeling even worse than she had been already, as if Alessia wasn't suffering enough. "Rebel, come." The big boxer followed her into the bedroom. She put him in his kennel and went back to join the others.

"Alessia, I'm sorry you have such strong allergies, but I really don't think you're in any danger," Mike said. "I spent a lot of time last night reading the file on the different murders. From what I can tell, the killer seems to target certain individuals rather than a certain vineyard. If he or she was targeting a vineyard, I can't help but think that someone else from that particular vineyard would have been murdered too."

Alessia smiled timidly. "Thanks, Mike. I hope your theory is correct."

"Me too." Mike scratched his temple. "Alessia, did you see Julie this morning before she went out to meditate and would you tell me her usual schedule in the mornings?"

"Yes. I saw her just as she was leaving. She was walking out of her bedroom, dressed in a sweat suit because the mornings here are a bit crisp this time of year. I was on my way to the bathroom, and she told me she'd see me in about an hour."

"I probably already know the answer to this, but did she seem any different to you than she usually did?"

"No, Mike. It was exactly like every other morning." Alessia turned and looked at Ted and said, "You'll back me up on this, right Ted? Julie never missed her morning meditation. I think everyone around her knew about it, and a lot of the other winery owners kidded her and said they should probably try it, so their winery could be as successful as the Lugano Winery."

For the first time Ted smiled. "No matter how late we'd been out the night before, and some of the galas here in the Napa and Sonoma area that as a sheriff I have to attend, can end up very late. Anyway, she was always up and out the door promptly at 6:30 to meditate. People even teased her at events, telling her it was time for us to leave, so she could meditate in the morning."

"Alessia, Ted, can either one of you think of anything that Julie did differently in the last week?" Mike asked. "Did she mention any phone calls? Did someone come here who normally didn't? Anything at all. Just take a minute and think about it."

Several minutes later, Ted spoke, his voice weary. "Mike, I've racked my brain and I can't think of one thing. Julie was very involved in the wine industry, and that was pretty much her life. As a matter of fact, about the only thing I can think of that she did unrelated to wine was meditate. She never mentioned, nor did I see, one thing that was any different."

Ted turned to Alessia. "You and Julie were practically joined at the hip. She told me many times that you were always with her, because she wanted you to know everything about the winery. Did you notice anything?"

"Like you, Ted, I've been racking my brain as well, and all that comes to mind are the daily aggravations like a problem with the bottling, or some vendor sold out of a certain wine, and we didn't have any more. Those are things that happen daily, but nothing was in the least bit out the ordinary. Aggravating, yes. Time-consuming, yes. Threatening, no. I wish I could be of more help, but I can't."

"Mike, I think we should give Alessia and the sheriff some time to themselves," Kevin said. "I don't have any more questions for them, and if you don't, I think they could both use a little private time. Okay with you?"

"Absolutely. Thank you for coming, and I'll be talking to both of you as the investigation proceeds. Alessia, I'm going to visit with the other wineries where a murder took place, but I think it would be a good idea if Kelly stayed here in case you need anything. She's had a little practice in this area, I'm sorry to say."

"I'm sure I won't need anything, but thanks. I do want to get a few things together before the lawyer comes, and I'm sure some of the staff will have questions and things that need seeing to," she said as she stood up, and left for what was now her house, the one that had been Julie's before she went outside to meditate earlier that morning.

"Mike, what are you going to look for at the other wineries?" Kevin asked. "I've spent extensive time at all of them and as you know from the file, I've come up with nothing."

Mike shrugged. "I'm sure my result will be the same, Kevin, but I like to get my own feel for things. I'll let you know if I find out anything." The three men stood up and Mike walked Ted and Kevin to the door. Before they left, he turned to Ted and said, "Sheriff, take care of yourself. I know it's become a lot more personal, but you have my word that I'll do everything in my power to find out who murdered Julie."

As they were on their way out, Kelly walked over to them and said, "Excuse me, Sheriff Dawson. May I have a word with you?"

"Of course, Kelly. Let's step over to my car. What can I do for you?"

"That nephew of yours, the dog trainer that law enforcement uses, is he from around here?" she asked.

"Sure is," he said with a smile. "Like I said, a lot of the law enforcement agencies that use dogs go to him. Why? Are you thinking you need another one?"

"No, I just have a thought. Could you give me his telephone number, and may I use your name?"

"I can do better than a number. Here's his card," he said as he removed it from his wallet. "After the winery owners started buying so many dogs from him, thought it would just be easier to give them his card when they asked, and of course you can use my name. Tell him I said hi, and we need to get together soon for a glass of wine."

CHAPTER THIRTEEN

"What was that all about?" Mike asked when Kelly walked back into the guest house.

"I'll let you know if it works out. I had a thought, and I want to see where it takes me."

"As long as it's not dangerous, I'll let you have it," he said with a grin. "Kelly, you heard me say I was going to visit the other winery owners today. I'm sure Kevin has done his due diligence on that front, but I'll feel better if I do it too. I'll probably be gone for several hours. You might want to see if you can help Alessia with anything."

"Was already planning on it," Kelly said. "It's hard enough when someone who's almost like a mother to you is murdered, and then compound that by suddenly becoming the owner of one of the best-known wineries in California. That's an awful lot to process on such short notice. She must be under a tremendous amount of pressure right now."

"I agree. Poor thing, and it doesn't look like she has anyone here who can help her. Somebody said the other winery owners would help, and I'm sure Sheriff Dawson will do whatever he can, so maybe that will be of some help to her. He seems close to the other owners, so he could probably exert some pressure on them, if needed."

"Yeah. Did you hear him say that his life is over? I know I'd sure feel that way if you were murdered," Mike said, as he put his arms around Kelly and lightly kissed her. "Don't put yourself in harm's way when I'm gone, hear me?"

"Loud and clear, Sheriff. I promise to do nothing more than stay here with Rebel and check in on Alessia. I'll be perfectly safe," she said.

"I'd like to say that sounds good, but I rather imagine Julie felt the same way this morning when she was on her own property, doing nothing more than going out for her usual morning meditation."

"Mike, you're the smart one in the family…" Kelly said.

He interrupted her. "I wish that were true, but continue."

Kelly chewed her lower lip. "Do you have any sense of commonality here? Is there anything other than being winery owners that these victims have in common?"

He stepped away from her as he considered her question. "Something's bothering me here, Kelly, and I think you've hit the nail on the head. It seems to me that there has to be some sort of a nexus between the people who were killed. Obviously, the murderer is targeting the owners of successful wineries, but why those particular wineries? I guess what I'm saying is that there are a lot of other very fine wineries in the Sonoma area, so why were the owners of these particular wineries targeted?

"If the killer wanted to do harm to a winery, why not kill some key employee like the field manager or some other person that's critical to the success of that winery? Instead the killer has exclusively targeted the owners. There has to be some common thread that links them together, but I haven't found it." He rubbed his chin.

"And here's another thing," he went on. "I think the killer is a man. The killer is an expert shot with a pistol. Each of the murdered individuals was killed with one single shot to the heart. As a general rule, men are usually more familiar with firearms than women, particularly in rural areas like Sonoma, where hunting is common. Also, I'm inclined to think the victims knew the killer. Take Julie for example. She was sitting at the top of a long sloping ridge, her back to a large oak tree, and her vision directed down the slope towards the winery.

"It's a long walk up that slope and unless she had her eyes closed the entire time the killer was walking up the slope, she must have seen the killer coming. Yet she did nothing to try and get away, stand up, or do anything, for that matter. She simply continued to sit next to the tree until the killer walked up to her and killed her with one single shot to her heart. To me that means she knew who the killer was, and she did nothing because she didn't think she was in any kind of a danger as the killer approached her.

"I can't figure out why a male suspect, who is an expert shot, and apparently known to his victims, is killing these winery owners, but, like you just said, I'm starting to think there must be some sort of common connection between all of them. I simply haven't been able to find that missing link."

"Know what, Sheriff, I'd be willing to bet everything I own you will." She shooed him away. "Now get out of here and do what you do best, catch a killer."

"I appreciate the vote of confidence, Kelly. I'll give you a call later and tell you how I'm doing."

"Mike, you have your gun on you, don't you?"

"Not only on me, but the last thing I was going to tell you before I left is the one I bought for you a while back is in my nightstand. I brought mine and yours with me on the plane. I'd rather be safe than sorry."

"See you later," she said, closing the door after Mike.

"Okay, Rebel," Kelly said as she let him out of his kennel, "time for you to commune with nature. Sorry I had to put you in your kennel this morning, but I didn't want Alessia to look any worse than she already did. We'll see if we can't take care of her problem later this morning."

They walked behind the house, and Rebel sauntered down a path between a row of grapevines. She looked up on the ridge where the sheriff's office was conducting its investigation and saw several men walking around the big oak tree, looking down at the ground. She hoped they found something that would be a clue to help identify the killer.

A few minutes later Rebel returned and they walked back to the guest house.

Even knowing murders are taking place here in the Sonoma area, it really has to be one of the most beautiful places I've ever seen, Kelly thought. *The word "murder" in this setting just doesn't fit.*

She took the card the sheriff had given her out of her pocket and punched the phone number on the card into her cell phone. A moment later a man's voice said, "Jim Dawson Canine Training. May I help you?"

"I hope so. My name's Kelly Reynolds. My husband is the sheriff of Beaver County, Oregon, and your uncle Ted called my husband to see if he could come down and help him with the Wine Country Killer case. My husband had helped him a while ago when we were visiting here on vacation."

"That was awfully nice of your husband. We need all the help we can get. Everyone is just waiting for the other shoe to drop, you know, another murder to be committed."

Kelly took a deep breath, and said, "I hate to tell you this, Jim, but it has. Julie Lugano was murdered this morning."

When Kelly didn't hear anything for several long moments, she said, "Hello? Jim, are you there?"

"Yes, I'm here. Sorry about that, but I can't believe what you just told me. Poor Ted. He was so devastated when my aunt died, all of us were really worried about him. Julie was a gift to him. He was so happy. That poor man doesn't deserve this. Do you know if he's at home or at work?"

"I believe he's at home, Jim. He was going to take a little time off."

"I'm only about twenty minutes away from his house. I'll go visit him right now. I'm sure he could use some company."

"I think family is just what he needs now, but I'd like to talk to you about something else. Julie Lugano's niece from Italy, Alessia, has been living with her for several years, and she's inheriting the winery and everything else that goes with it. My husband and I have a guard dog, a boxer, we brought with us, and I suggested it might be a good idea for Julie to keep him with her until the murderer was found.

"She's by herself, and although they have a security guard here, obviously it wasn't enough to help Julie, and now Alessia's in that large house by herself. Unfortunately, she's highly allergic to dogs, so she rejected my offer. Here's my question. Would you happen to have trained any guard dogs for people who have allergies? I know that's kind of a strange question, but although I've read that poodles and Portuguese water dogs are good breeds for people with allergies, I've never heard that they made good guard dogs, even with their intelligence."

"Kelly, this is probably going to surprise you, but I've found that Giant Schnauzers are great dogs for people who have allergies, but want a guard dog. Alessia's not the only one who's allergic to dogs. Trust me, a lot of people in the police and military have allergies. The breed is great for that purpose, because they guard both their master and their territory."

"That sounds just like what she needs. Can you give me some names of trainers who might have one? I imagine there aren't too many around, because they seem a little out of the ordinary for guard dogs. Most people think of German shepherds or Doberman pinschers, and the like."

"I can do better than that. I have one who is a year old that I've been training. I was about ready to call a couple of police agencies who always buy my dogs and tell them that that I have a fully trained dog that would be perfect for an officer with allergies. Whenever I do that, I sell the dog immediately. Casey, that's what I've named this dog, is ready to be placed. Alessia could have him now, if that works."

"Talk about a coincidence. I'm not usually fond of them, but in this case, it will work perfectly. I'm staying in the guest house at the Lugano Winery. I'll be here for several hours. Is there any chance you could bring Casey here, as well as his food, and other paraphernalia? Naturally, I'll pay you for Casey and everything else."

"Actually, this is on me. I would have sent a flower arrangement, and this will just be in lieu of it. It would make me feel good to know I'm doing something to help the niece of the woman who my uncle loved. Casey and I will be over there within the hour."

CHAPTER FOURTEEN

Forty-five minutes later a van with the words "Jim Dawson Canine Training" pulled up in front of the guest house. Kelly had been eagerly looking out the window in anticipation of meeting the new addition to the winery. As soon as the van stopped, she hurried outside to greet Jim and Casey.

"Hi, you must be Kelly. I'm Jim Dawson," the broad sandy-haired man said as he stepped out of the van, walked over to her, and held his hand out. Kelly thought the family genes must be strong, because there was definitely a resemblance between Jim and his uncle, Sheriff Dawson.

"Jim, I can't tell you how much I appreciate you doing this. I called Alessia a few minutes ago to make sure she was home. She was just ending a meeting with her lawyer and said she planned on staying in the house the rest of the afternoon. She said she needed to make a number of telephone calls, one being to your uncle to help her plan Julie's funeral."

Jim walked to the back of the van and opened the rear doors. "Come, Casey," he said, and a beautiful black dog jumped out of the van, walked over to where Jim was, and sat down next to him. "Casey, this is Kelly." The dog turned and looked at her.

"Kelly, put your hand out so he can smell it." Kelly did and a moment later the big dog put his paw up, as if shaking her hand. "There, now you've officially been introduced. I'd like him to meet Alessia before I get his gear out. Think it's okay to go over there now? I've met her before at parties my uncle had, so I don't think she'll be shocked to see me."

As they were speaking the door to Julie's house opened, and Alessia held the door open as a man walked out. She saw Kelly and waved and then saw Jim and Casey. She walked over to them.

"Alessia, I'm so sorry about your aunt," Jim said. "I'm on my way over to my uncle's now, but I have a gift for you suggested by Kelly. I think it will do you far more good than a large flower arrangement that would probably end up in a nursing home the day after the funeral. Kelly wanted you to have this hypoallergenic guard dog."

He reached down and scratched Casey's ears. "Casey, meet your new owner, Alessia Lugano."

Alessia stood stock still, not knowing quite what to do. For a moment Kelly began to doubt the wisdom of her action, thinking that one more thing for Alessia might just be too much, but Casey deftly took charge. He walked over to his new master and sat down beside her. She put her hand down to pet him and he put his paw up, as if in greeting.

"You're a beauty and obviously well-trained, but Jim, as I told Kelly I'm highly allergic to dogs." She looked down at her hand and said, "That's weird, usually when I pet a dog I immediately get a rash, and whenever I'm near one my eyes start watering. I'm not doing that now."

"Alessia, I know English is your second language and you may not know know the word 'hypoallergenic.' In English it means that something is unlikely to cause you to have an allergic reaction to it."

"Jim, are you saying I could be around this dog and not have an allergic reaction?" Alessia's expression relaxed. "I've always had allergic reactions when I'm around dogs."

"Well, judging by the way you look now, I think we can assume that you can safely be around Casey. I've brought his dog bed, a leash, and some food which will last for a week or so, as well as detailed instructions on what foods he can have, commands he's trained to obey, and everything you need to know.

"When Kelly and I spoke, she asked me if I knew of any guard dogs for people who are allergic to dogs. I train this breed for law enforcement agencies who have people with allergies. In other words, he's a fully trained guard dog, and has been trained in both verbal and hand sign commands, all of which I've included in his instructions."

"Kelly, you did all this for me in this short time?" Alessia asked, clearly shocked that it had happened so quickly. "You heard what Kevin said, that there had been no problems at the other wineries where someone had been murdered."

'Yes, I did, and evidently, he's been right, but I did it for your peace of mind. I'm sure there won't be any incidences, and now you won't need to worry every time you hear a wall creak in the wind or some other strange sound in the house. Keep Casey with you at all times. From what Jim said, this breed is known for guarding its master as well as its territory, and I think you and the winery are now both to him."

"Alessia, could we go in the house and I'll give you some more instructions and demonstrate how to properly give commands to Casey?" Jim asked. "Since you've never had a dog before, it's going to sound a little strange when I tell you that Casey should sleep in your bedroom with you. His bed can go anywhere in there, but please believe me, when I tell you that you're a lot safer with him than you would be with a loaded gun. These dogs put their life in harm's way for the people they protect."

"Well, Casey, I guess it's you and me now," Alessia said with a friendly smile. "Might as well introduce you to your new surroundings and get you situated." Alessia turned to Kelly and said, "Thank you. I never would have thought to do something like this on my own. It's funny, but I've always envied people who had dogs, and particularly well-trained ones. It never occurred to me that I could be one of those people. You've provided a ray of sunshine on what has to be the darkest day of my life. Jim, Kelly, Casey, let's go." The three of them, along with Casey, turned and headed towards the main house.

Okay, I know this is the most inappropriate time ever for a thought like this, but wouldn't it be wonderful if Jim and Alessia began to bond over Casey? They're about the same age, neither one is married, or at least he wasn't wearing a wedding ring, and she could sure use some masculine help now.

The thought had no sooner crossed her mind than Kelly mentally chided herself for even thinking something like that. Even so, she couldn't shake it. Good things often came out of bad ones, and you just never know what the future's going to hold.

CHAPTER FIFTEEN

While Jim was giving instructions to Alessia about the proper care and feeding of Casey, Kelly called Sheriff Dawson.

"Hi, Ted, it's Kelly Reynolds. Just wanted to fill you in on a couple of things." She told him about calling Jim and getting Casey for Alessia.

"Kelly, I'm so glad you did that. Wish I'd thought of it. She's got to be scared to death, given everything that's happened. Jim's dogs are the best. He called a little while ago and told me he was coming over to see me, but he had to make a stop on the way here. Didn't know the stop would involve you and Alessia.

"I'm going to be coming over to Alessia's later this afternoon," Ted went on. "She asked if I would help her plan the funeral, and of course, I told her yes. I was planning on having the winery patrolled hourly by a sheriff's car, since the security that was there when Julie was murdered…" His voice broke and he struggled for a moment to get himself under control.

He resumed speaking and said, "Anyway, I think a guard dog will be far better for her than any sheriff's car or security guard. My nephew has an incredible gift for training dogs. It's kind of weird. My brother and I noticed it when he was just a little kid. Whenever a dog was around it would go over to him, and a few minutes later the dog would do whatever Jim wanted. We nicknamed him The Dog Whisperer. He certainly found his calling at an early age."

"He seems like a fine young man. I'm sure your brother is very proud of him."

"I'm sure he would be if he were around. Unfortunately, my brother and his wife were sailing to Hawaii on a private ocean-going yacht when they encountered a severe storm and were lost at sea. Jim was in his early twenties then, and I've pretty much been a surrogate father for him ever since. My wife and I never had children, so I consider him to be the son I never had. We're very close."

"Well, whatever part you had in raising him was definitely successful. I'm glad you have him. I think he and Alessia will both be very good for you in the next few months."

"Yeah, probably, but I have to tell you I'm dreading facing the future without Julie. I think it's time for me to retire. I mean, if I couldn't find out who killed the vintners, and I couldn't even save my fiancée, what kind of a sheriff am I? Not a very good one, in my book."

Kelly picked up on his anguish from the other end of the line. "Ted, don't make any decisions about anything right now. Let things settle for a while."

"Probably good advice. By the way, Kelly, if you have time, could you sit in on the meeting Alessia and I are going to have about Julie's funeral? I'm aware you really didn't know Julie that well, and you don't know the other vintners and people in town, but I think just having you there would be good for Alessia. Since you got her the dog, she knows that you have her well-being at heart."

"Of course. I'd be happy to, although I rather doubt there's much I can do. What time are you two getting together?"

"I told her I'd be there about 3:00 this afternoon. Does that work for you?"

Kelly thought for a second and then said, "Yes, I think Mike told you he was spending the day going to the different wineries where murders have occurred to see if he can find out anything new about the cases. I don't expect him back until late this afternoon and then we're going to dinner at the second restaurant where you made reservations for us.

"With everything that happened today, I don't think we had a chance to tell you how good the dinner was that we had last night. I mean it was superb, and thanks not only for the wine but also for picking up the dinner tab. That was really kind of you. Thanks again."

"Glad you enjoyed it. In my opinion, Giovanni's is one of the best restaurants around. I'll be curious what you think of the one where you're going tonight."

"I'll definitely let you know. See you later, Ted."

Kelly spent the rest of the afternoon checking emails, calling Roxie to find out how Kelly's Koffee Shop was doing, and calling her daughter, Julia, to see what was new with her and her husband, Brad, as well as her two loveable granddaughters. They were growing up so fast, she never liked to go long without hearing about their latest milestones.

CHAPTER SIXTEEN

Later that afternoon, Kelly heard Ted's car pull up and stop in front of Julie's house. She walked out to meet him and together the two of them walked up to the front door of the main house and knocked. "Who is it?" Alessia asked a moment later.

"It's Ted and Kelly, Alessia."

The door opened and Alessia gave Ted a hug while Casey stood looking at him. Since she'd hugged him, Casey was calm, but Kelly had the feeling that if there had been any hesitancy on her part, Casey would have assumed command of the situation.

"And who do we have here?" Ted asked as he knelt down and petted the big dog. Casey looked him over before seeking reassurance from Alessia who nodded, and then he put his right paw up. Ted, smiling, met his paw with a gentle fist bump. "Well, I can see that my nephew has done his usual good job with this one." Ted rose to his feet. "What do you think, Alessia?"

"Quite honestly, Ted, I'd give anything if I'd gotten Casey under different circumstances, but now that I have him, I couldn't be happier. And quite frankly, it's not just the guard dog thing. He's just a great companion. It may get old in the future, but right now it makes me feel very comfortable to have this guy with me everywhere I go.

"I've drawn the line at the bathroom. I close the door, but when I open it, he's laying right in front of it. That might take some getting used to. Let's go in the kitchen and I'll get us some coffee, or if you'd like I have the inside track to some great wines."

"Coffee for me," Kelly said. "We're going out to dinner tonight so I'll save my alcohol ration for that."

"I'll take coffee as well," Ted said.

"Ted, I'd like you to be very involved in everything having to do with Julie's funeral," Alessia said, when she'd finished preparing the coffee and they were seated around the old wooden kitchen table. "As you know, Julie and I are, were, Catholic. I've talked to Father Damon and if it's all right with you, I'd like to have the funeral as soon as possible.

"I don't like long drawn-out times between deaths and funerals. He said we could have a morning funeral with Mass the day after tomorrow. I told him that was fine, but I wanted to dispense with the vigil. Given the way she died, and so many others have suffered a similar fate, I think it would become a maudlin thing. What do you think?"

"I agree," Ted said. "I can get the word out to members of the wine industry. Why don't you call the Sonoma Index-Tribune and have them publish the details?"

"I'll do that when you leave. I was thinking about having something here at the winery after the service. Father Damon said we could have the service at 10:30 in the morning. The church is in town and then I thought people could come here afterwards."

She looked at Kelly and said, "Here in Sonoma, it's traditional to have wine served after a funeral. I'll have Ginger make up some small plates, and we can hold it in the wine tasting room. We'll close it to the public until later that afternoon. Do you think that would work?"

"Knowing how much Julie loved this winery and how much of

her is invested in it, I think having a celebration of her life here would be exactly what she would want," Kelly said.

Alessia turned to the sheriff. "Ted, Father Damon wanted to know if she was to be cremated or buried, and quite frankly, I didn't know what to say. Do you know what Julie's wishes would have been?"

He was quiet for a moment, and then he said, "When Mario died, it was his wish to be cremated and Julie did that. I know some spouses want to be buried with their husband or wife, but since that's not possible in this case, I think having her cremated would be fine. She must have been okay with that, or she would have had Mario buried."

"All right, I'll call him and tell him what we've decided."

"Wait a minute, Alessia. The decisions are yours. As you know, Julie and I were planning on getting married, but legally, you're far closer to her than I am. I have no claim."

Alessia reached out and placed her hand on Ted's arm. "No Ted, you're wrong, you have the claim of the heart, and that trumps everything."

Ted put his head down for a moment and when he looked up tears coursed down his cheeks as he said, "Thank you for that, Alessia. It means more to me than you'll ever know."

Alessia nodded and swallowed before continuing. Kelly suspected the young woman was also trying to contain her emotions. "I think that about finishes up the major things, but Ted, I'd like you to go to the church with me tomorrow." Alessia gave him a beseeching glance, her bottom lip trembling as she spoke.

"Father Damon wants me to choose the memorial funeral program. We'll have to decide the wording, whether we want photos, and if so, which ones. I was thinking of a photo of Julie overlaying one of the winery. What do you think of that?"

"It would be fitting." Ted's eyes shone through his tears. "Her life was this winery, so yes, I think that's totally appropriate. I'm sure people who don't live in the wine country might have a hard time understanding a program like that, but the people who will be attending her funeral will definitely understand. Do you have the photos?"

"I have one of Julie in my bedroom that I think is the best photo I've ever seen of her. The photo of the winery that's on the menu in the tasting room is excellent. With your permission, I'd like to use those."

"Alessia, you don't need my permission, but you honor me by asking. Now, let's talk about the operation of the winery for a minute. Do you want me to call a couple of the vintners and ask them to help you or are you comfortable making the decisions on your own? I only ask that because this is such a difficult time for you. Julie told me several times that she knew if anything ever happened to her, that you were fully capable of running the winery."

"Thanks, Ted, but I think I'm okay. We have a great staff, and Julie always included me in everything related to the winery. I'm sure there will be all kinds of things in the future that I will probably want help with, but for now, I'm fairly comfortable making any decisions that need to be made. I hope you don't mind if I use you as a sounding board before I call anyone else."

"Of course not, but I'm not a vintner. Sure, I've been around wineries all my life, and I've learned a lot over the years, but I've never been a vintner. Give me a call when you have any questions, and we'll decide who best to call."

Kelly looked at her watch. "I imagine Mike will be getting home soon, and I'm anxious to see what he's found out. I think you two have everything under control, not that I did anything anyway, so I'm going to leave you in Casey's capable paws. Alessia, give us a call if you need anything tonight."

"Thanks for coming over, and thanks for Casey. I'm already

attached to him. See you tomorrow."

"Enjoy dinner tonight, Kelly. It's pretty much a toss-up whether the restaurant you ate at last night is my favorite or whether tonight's choice is," Ted said.

CHAPTER SEVENTEEN

Kelly returned to the guest house, fed Rebel, and took him for a short walk. When they got back Mike was just driving into the parking area in front of the guest house. She and Rebel walked over to his car to greet him as Mike climbed out of the car. "Well, Kelly, how did the rest of your day go? Hope it was better than the beginning of the day."

"It was. I'll tell you all about it when we get inside and then I want to hear about the wineries and if you found out anything that can help." A few minutes later Kelly said, "We've got a little time before our dinner reservation. Let's catch up on what we each did today. I'll start." She told him about Casey, the new furry addition to the Lugano Winery, and the meeting she had with Ted and Alessia regarding the funeral arrangements.

"Mike, I really liked Ted's nephew, Jim, and I think he'll be someone Ted and possibly Alessia can lean on. From what he told me, his relationship with Ted is kind of a father-son thing. Evidently Jim's parents died when he was in his early twenties. I'd like you to meet him. He's really nice."

"Good. Ted's going to need somebody to provide a little moral support for him. All of the people I met with today expressed their concern about Ted regarding Julie's death. He's very well-liked and everyone said that he and Julie had a wonderful relationship. It's going to be rough for him."

"I'm not surprised. He was pretty broken up several times today, but Alessia seems to be handling it well. She's relying on Ted and that should make him feel needed. She seems very capable. I just hope she's up to the task of running the winery, although Ted seemed to think that the other vintners were more than ready to help her if and when she needed it."

Inside, Kelly paused in the hallway. "I'm thirsty, but I want to save my daily wine allotment for dinner. Join me in a cup of tea?"

"Sounds great. While you're getting it, I'll change clothes. Have you fed Rebel?"

"Are you kidding? Do you really think he would let this time of evening go by without his dinner?" Kelly chuckled and petted Rebel, whose ears had pricked up at the sound of his name. "Yes, fed and taken for his early evening constitutional. Back in a minute," she said as she walked towards the kitchen to make the tea.

A few minutes later she walked into the great room where Mike, who had changed clothes and combed his hair, was seated in one of the armchairs. She handed him a cup of tea. "Here you be, Sheriff. Now tell me all about the wineries you visited today."

"Thanks, Kelly. This hits the spot," Mike said as he took a sip. He set it down on the table and said, "I decided to start by visiting the wineries in the order that the vintners had been murdered. I wanted to see if I could pick up some kind of a pattern that Ted may have missed because he knows them so well. The first one I went to was the Neri Winery."

"Mike, were these wineries located close together or far apart? Was there any order to the distancing of them?"

"No, good thought, but no. The Neri Winery is only about a mile from here. I met with the new owner of the winery, Joseph Larson, and the manager of the vineyard. Joseph bought it from the Neri family. As you may remember from our briefing, Riccardo Neri was the owner. His widow had no desire to run it and decided to sell it. The vineyard manager was the one who discovered Riccardo's body, but he had nothing to add to what was already in the file. Bottom line, I didn't find out anything new."

"I don't think this, but I'll throw it out," Kelly said. "Since this Joseph guy bought the winery and given the timing, seems like it was sold in a timely manner. In other words, it didn't sit on the market for years so the Neri widow could get top dollar. If that's the case, any inkling that the Joseph guy could have had something to do with the murder, so he could pick up the winery at a good price?"

"You've been around me too long. I thought the same thing and rather directly asked him about how he found out about the property being for sale. He's some stockbroker genius from New York who made a bundle, always loved this part of the United States, and had a realtor advising him when wine properties came on the market. He'd been looking for several years, and when his realtor told him about this one, he made an offer, and it was accepted. By the way, he was in New York at the time of the murder."

"So, you're saying you don't think he had anything to do with the Neri murder?" Kelly asked.

"I am. He gave me the name and number of his realtor and while I was on my way to the HaJam Winery I called her. She told me he had come to Sonoma several times to look at properties and they were either too large, too commercial, wanted too much money, or he didn't have a good feel towards it. He'd been waiting in the wings for the right place for a while.

"She said the Neri Winery, with its superb reputation and boutique size, fit his requirements, and he fell in love with the winery as soon as he saw it. He made an offer within an hour of touring it, and in the shortest escrow time possible, he was the new owner. Seems like just a series of common events, nothing sinister."

"One down. And the HaJam winery?"

"Pretty much a repeat of what I've just said. The main difference is this winery is about ten miles north of town. I met with the new owner and the vineyard manager. Again, nothing out of the ordinary. I talked with the woman who found the two victims, the maid, who always cleaned the room where they did their tasting the day afterward. Just as was the case with all the others there were no prints, no clues, no signs of struggle."

"Mike, are you still thinking the victims knew the murderer? I mean there have been four incidences of murder, although five people have been killed, but I don't believe I've heard anything about a struggle, signs on the body that there was a struggle, or anything like that. What do you think?"

"Yes. I've pretty much decided the victims all knew the killer, and they must have known the person well, since there aren't any signs of a struggle."

"Seems to me that indicates that the murderer is someone who lives in Sonoma or travels here regularly. Would you agree?"

"Yes, and I specifically asked everyone I spoke to if there were any new people who had come to the winery before or after the murders. In every case, the answer was no."

"Okay, that takes care of two more of the victims and of course there is Julie's murder, but I was there when you talked to people about it, so I don't think we need to go over that again. I believe there was one more murder. Right?"

"Yes. It was Nicola Ferlante of the Ferlante Winery. His winery is one of the first ones you see when you drive north out of Sonoma, so no nexus with the distances of the different wineries. I talked to his wife, Anna, who is now the sole owner of the winery, Lucia, who was his assistant in the tasting room, and the vineyard manager. Nothing to tell. Anna was the one who found him when he was late getting back from the tasting room. She'd been involved in a lot of the winery business, so she felt fairly confident that she could run it. From what I could tell, she has the undying loyalty of everyone at the winery."

Kelly paused and then said, "You know I subscribe to a lot of cooking and restaurant magazines. While I know next to nothing about wine other than whether I like one or not, recently there have been a number of articles about women vintners and the increasing number of them working in the industry."

"That may be true, but I don't think Anna took over the winery for that reason. She and Nicola, or Nick as she called him, have two children. She told me it had been Nick's dream to have their son, Leonardo, take over the winery just as Nick had taken it over from his father, Paolo."

"How old is Leonardo?" Kelly asked.

"He's twelve, so it looks like Anna will be running it for several more years."

She thought about what Mike had told her and said, "How sad. So really, other than confirming what Ted and Kevin told you, and what's in the file, you didn't learn anything new."

"That's true, but I don't consider it a wash. It simply backs up what they and the file said. If I hadn't done my own due diligence, I'd always wonder if they'd missed something." Mike rubbed his chin. "The problem is, I'm not exactly sure where to go now. I want to talk to the sheriff's deputies who conducted the investigation today at the location where Julie was murdered and see what they found out. Maybe the key to solving this mystery will come to me in a dream tonight. I could sure use some help about now, even if it's in a dream."

"I think what you need is a good dinner, and Ted has already made reservations for us at his other favorite restaurant. Give me just a minute to change clothes, and I'll be ready."

"Go ahead. I'll look at the news and see what they have to say about Julie's murder." He picked up the remote control and pointed it at the television set in the corner.

CHAPTER EIGHTEEN

"There it is, Mike. LaSalette. It's a Portuguese restaurant. Matter of fact, this will be a first for me. I don't think I've ever eaten Portuguese food."

"I've had it a time or two. As I remember, they eat a lot of cod. Before I met you, there was a sheriff in the next county over who became a good friend of mine. He's retired now, but his wife was Portuguese, and I used to go there for dinner once in a while. Good food. I think we're in for a treat. Well, that's serendipitous. A car just pulled out in front of the restaurant, and I can take that spot."

"Serendipitous is just a fancy word for a coincidence, and I know what you think of coincidences," Kelly said with a smile and a teasing tone.

"I prefer to use the word 'serendipitous.' Sounds a lot classier and more like when something good happens."

"Have it your way," Kelly said as she got out of the car. They walked the few steps to the restaurant, Mike holding the door open for his wife and placing his hand in the small of her back as they entered. He gave Ted's name to the attractive woman at the front desk and a moment later they followed her through the restaurant to the enclosed patio area.

"I know it's a little cool tonight, but Sheriff Dawson wanted you to experience the courtyard," the hostess explained. "We have outdoor heaters, so I think you'll be very comfortable here. Enjoy your meal and please tell Sheriff Dawson how sorry we are about Julie. They were regulars here, and we're all taking his loss very personally."

"I certainly will, and I'm sure it will mean a great deal to him," Mike said. She gave each of them a menu and walked away. Mike reached into his pocket to put his cell phone on the table. It wasn't there. He looked in his sport coat inside pocket, his front pants pockets, and even his back pocket.

"What are you doing?" Kelly asked.

"Darn it. I must have left my phone on the dresser when I changed clothes. I really hate to be without it."

"Actually, it's probably a blessing in disguise. It will force you to relax for a little while." Kelly looked around the space, which was bathed in a lustrous glow. "Mike, this is like a fairyland. Everywhere you look something's glittering, from the candles to the twinkling lights that are on every branch of every tree here in the courtyard. And did you look around when we came through the restaurant? Absolutely beautiful. I particularly like the touch of real paintings on the walls rather than the prints you usually see."

"This is just what I need after a day like today. Let's look at the menu and see what appeals to us." At that moment the wine steward appeared with a bottle of wine and wine glasses.

"Sheriff Reynolds, Mrs. Reynolds, this is a thank you from Sheriff Dawson. It's a 1997 red wine from the Ramos Pintos Winery in Porto. I think you'll like it. It's his favorite Portuguese wine." He poured Mike a small amount and waited for him to taste it.

"That's excellent, thank you," Mike said as the wine steward poured each of them a glass.

"Enjoy. Your server will be with you in a moment."

"Mike, I rarely do this, but I'm in way over my head here, having never had this type of food. I'm thinking of asking our server to choose for us. Would that by okay with you?" Kelly asked.

"Considering I would have no idea what I'd be ordering either, I think it's an excellent idea. Consider it done."

A few minutes later a young man, wearing a white shirt and black slacks, walked up to their table. "Good evening. My name is Gustavo. I will be serving you tonight. Have you had a chance to look over the menu?"

Kelly looked up at him and smiled. "We have and since neither of us knows anything about this type of food, we'd like you to select for us. Can you do that?"

"It would be my pleasure. I would start off with the Tasca Board. It has São Jorge cheese, Serrano ham, linguica, which is a type of sausage, and rillettes, which is a meat spread and pickles. It's enough for two people, and of course bread and crackers are served with it. I would follow it with the heirloom salad. Again, you can split that."

"Yes, that sounds great. What would you suggest for the main course?" Kelly asked.

"Since you're not familiar with Portuguese food, I would suggest you each get something different. I will bring extra plates and you can share your entrées. Would that work for you?"

Mike nodded. "I think that's a great idea. So, what are we having?"

"For you sir, a very traditional dish, a casserole of north Atlantic salted cod with potatoes, onions, and olives." He turned towards Kelly, "I think you would enjoy the fisherman's stew. It consists of sea bass, scallops, clams, mussels, shrimp, potatoes, and linguica. We can discuss dessert when you've finished the entrée."

"Sounds great, Gustavo. We're in your capable hands," Mike said.

"Very good sir. I'll be back shortly with the Tasca Board."

When they'd finished sharing the appetizer, the salad, and their entrées, Kelly said, "This was a wonderful choice. Considering there's not a speck of food on any of our plates, I'd say we enjoyed it."

"I did more than enjoy it. That was one of the best meals I've ever had and the ambience certainly adds to it. What are we going to do for dessert?" Mike asked.

"Change that to what are you going to do for dessert. I'm so full, I couldn't eat another bite."

"I see you enjoyed my recommendations," Gustavo said when he returned to clear their table. "I am glad. For dessert, may I suggest the cinnamon vanilla bean flan with a caramel glaze. It's absolutely addictive, and I think the best thing on the menu."

"I would like that," Mike said. "My wife is full, so just bring one."

"Actually, make it two," Kelly said quickly, before Gustavo turned away. "I think my dessert pocket just opened."

"Very well, and may I suggest a glass of port to go with it?" Gustavo asked.

"No, thank you. I think we've both had enough for tonight."

"Certainly, I'll be back in a moment." Gustavo turned and walked towards the kitchen.

"Kelly, your dessert pocket? That's one I haven't heard," Mike said, with a bemused look on his face.

"Well, once in a while I sacrifice and open it up. I think tonight is a good time to do it.

"Uh-huh. I'm sure Gustavo is amusing the kitchen help with that."

"Whatever. The flan just sounded too good to pass up."

CHAPTER NINETEEN

"Mike, I'm so glad I didn't pass up the flan. It was fabulous. Hands down, the best I've ever had," Kelly said as they headed back to the guest house in the car Ted had provided for Mike.

"I agree. Everything was excellent. I'll call Ted in the morning and thank him. I'm not sure I would have ever chosen a Portuguese restaurant on my own, but I certainly will in the future."

"Agreed. What's on your agenda for tomorrow?"

"I don't have anything specific. I've been thinking about what's next. I've decided to talk to all of the sheriff's personnel who investigated the murders. Maybe by talking to them I might find a common thread which was overlooked when they investigated each murder separately. Other than that, I don't have much to go on. It's very frustrating. I don't think I'm doing Ted much good."

Kelly turned towards him. "I completely disagree. Given what happened this morning, there is no way he could have overseen the investigation, even if his lead investigator is Kevin. It was a good thing you were here."

"That's probably true, and you? What are you doing tomorrow?"

"Alessia asked me if I would help her with some of the

arrangements for the funeral. For whatever reason, maybe because I represent some sort of mother figure to her, she'd like me to help her pick out something to wear for the church service. She also wanted to talk to me about what to serve at the reception. The woman in charge of the tasting room, Ginger, and a few people who are on staff are going to do whatever prep they can prior to the funeral.

"The tasting room serves some small plates along with the wines and they have a full commercial kitchen, so that should work out well," Kelly continued. "At least Alessia won't have to go to the expense and worry of hiring a caterer, and in a town that's this involved in both food and wine, it might be difficult to find one on such short notice."

"Good. I'm glad you can help her, and although I haven't met him yet, that was a brilliant idea of yours, to get Casey for her. I can see some lights on over at her house, but it looks like she doesn't feel she needs to have a light on in every room. She must feel comfortable having Casey there with her." After he'd parked the car and they'd entered the guest house, Mike walked back towards the bedroom.

"Rebel, time to go outside one more time for the night," Kelly said. "Come on, I'll take you. Mike, Rebel and I are going out for a few minutes," Kelly called to him. "Be back in a few."

"Okay. Found my phone just where I left it. There's a message for me to call Ted. I'll join you when I'm through."

Kelly walked Rebel to the far end of the parking lot where a grassy area was located. A few minutes later, when they returned to the house, she heard Mike on the phone. She walked into the bedroom and he made a sign with his fingers squeezed together that he'd just be a few more minutes.

He ended the call and said, "Kelly, I'm sorry, but I have to go over to Ted's house right away. Evidently one of the vintners called him and wants to meet with him. He's on his way over to Ted's right now, and Ted wants me to join them. I have no idea what this is all about."

Kelly pursed her lips. "Good grief, Mike. It's 9:30. Isn't that a little late for a meeting? Couldn't it wait until tomorrow?"

"I guess not. Ted's as much in the dark as I am, but the man, his name is Mason Bryant, of the Bryant Vineyards, said he thinks he knows something that will help in the investigation of the murders. After all, that's what I'm here for, so I really don't have a choice. Go to bed, and I'll wake you when I get back and tell you what it was all about."

"Okay. Be safe. See you later."

*****

Mike followed the directions Ted had given him and ten minutes later he pulled up in front of a charming white Spanish style single story house with a red tile roof. Even though it was nighttime, Mike couldn't miss the riot of color crated by the plantings in front of the house. He maintained that he had a brown thumb and knew very little about plants, but even he could appreciate the peonies, iris, and delphiniums that were growing in abundance in front of the house. There were several other types of plants that were just as beautiful, but he didn't know what they were.

He knocked on the door and it was immediately opened by Ted. "Ted, your flowers are beautiful. You must have an incredible green thumb. Kelly would love to see them. I must bring her by."

"Thanks for coming on such short notice, Mike. Come in, and yes, gardening is a hobby of mine. Probably doesn't go with the tough guy sheriff image, but it was a passion of my wife's and when she died, I vowed to keep her memory alive through it."

"Well, I'm sure she would appreciate it. It really is spectacular."

Ted gestured for Mike to follow him and they walked down a hall into a room Mike assumed was his office. A man was sitting in a leather club chair and stood up when Mike and Ted walked into the room. "Mike, I want you to meet Mason Bryant. He's the owner of the Bryant Winery that produces some of the best red blends to come out of Sonoma. I think even Mason has forgotten the number of awards he's won with his wines. They really are spectacular."

Ted turned to the other man, who was tall and tanned, with dark hair and hooded eyes. "Mason, this is Mike Reynolds. He's the sheriff of Beaver County, Oregon. Remember when the winemaster, Angela, at the Moretti Winery, was murdered and her body was found in a wine vat? Well, Mike helped solve the murder, along with a lot of help from his wife. As you know, I asked them to come here and give me hand with the Wine Country Killer case. You were gracious enough to send your plane for them. Please, both of you, sit down."

Ted walked around his desk and sat down while Mike and Mason sat across from him. "Okay, Mason, what have you come up with?"

"Like everyone else around here, I've been racking my brain trying to come up with why certain vintners have been murdered and why others haven't," Mason began. "All of the ones who have been murdered are vintners who produce excellent wines, but there are other vintners in the area who do the same."

"I agree," Ted said. "That very thought has kept me awake many a night."

"Another thing. Why just Sonoma vintners? Why not Napa vintners?" Mason raked a hand through his hair. "If anything, Napa is probably better known than Sonoma for wine, certainly in a commercial form. And geographically, Napa and Sonoma are very close to each other, separated by about ten or fifteen miles. So why not target some Napa vintners for murder, since they're so close by? But that hasn't happened.

"That left me, and as I'm sure, both of you, with the thought that there must be something the vintners who were murdered had in common or shared, and it must be something to do with Sonoma. I've gone through family ties, education, location, etcetera. I had pretty much decided maybe it was someone who was jealous of male vintners because no women had been murdered."

"Until today," Ted said softly.

"Yes, Ted, until today. And while I'm sick about Julie's death, and I've already told you how sorry I am about your lost future with her, her murder broke the mold of no woman having been murdered."

"I wish I could say that was a help, but obviously I'm not seeing what you're seeing," Ted said.

Mason took a deep breath. "I spent several hours in my office early this evening. I wrote down the names of each of the victims, their wineries, their awards, you name it. For the first time I came up with something they all shared." He looked expectantly at both of them.

"What did you find?" Mike asked, not sure if Ted was capable of speaking as emotionally raw as he was at the moment.

"Hear me out Ted, because I know you've heard of the Brotherhood of the Knights of Wine."

"Of course. It's the most prestigious group of wine connoisseurs in the United States," Ted said, "but what does that have to do with the murders? To my knowledge, they've never had an event in Sonoma. They always go to some fancy resort."

"I'm sorry to be the stupid one here," Mike said, "but I've never heard of it. If you think it's important, would you please fill me in?"

"Of course, and I think it's very important," Mason said. "It's an exclusive group of wealthy wine connoisseurs. To join the group the entry price is $10,000 and that's just the starting point. Another requirement for membership is that you must attend at least eight Brotherhood events in a five-year period, and as Ted mentioned, they are only held at high-end resorts throughout the United States, Alaska, and Hawaii. They've been around for at least thirty years that I know of."

"Is it difficult to become a member?" Mike asked.

"Yes. Not only is an applicant vetted for their financial ability to be a member in good standing, but they are also voted on by a membership committee. I have heard that only ten percent of the people who apply are accepted. They do the whole ritual thing when someone is initiated into the Brotherhood. It's a tradition rather than anything sinister.

"The person being initiated wears a red robe, which represents red wines, along with a pale white braided neckpiece, which represents white wines and the president of the Brotherhood presents each of them with their own sterling silver tasting cup. That's just after he touches their shoulders with a sabrage."

"I've always told my deputies that no question is dumb, so what is a sabrage? I have no idea what it is," Mike said.

"It's a small sword that was used to open champagne bottles and became popular in Napoleon's time in France," Mason explained. "The person using it smashes the blade of the sword into the neck of the bottle and the entire top of the glass champagne bottle is sheared off. It's pretty much just used for show and ritual now, which is why the group does it."

"Thanks. The things you learn in this business."

Ted interjected, "Mason, this is all interesting, and I knew some of this, but I fail to see why it's important in the Wine Country Killer case."

Mason leaned forward, his expression earnest. "Ted, I don't know if it is. I make wine. You catch the bad guys. This is your area of expertise, but I do think I've found a nexus and the Brotherhood is it. As you both know, I have a private plane. Three years ago, the Brotherhood selected the Wine Growers Association of Sonoma to showcase Sonoma wines at their biannual convention, which was going to be held at the Broadmoor Hotel in Colorado Springs, Colorado.

"They asked the Neri Winery, the HaJam Winery, the Lugano

Winery, the Ferlante Winery, and the Bryant Winery to come to the convention and bring cases of their wine for their members to sample." His eyes widened. "Believe me, being asked to showcase your wines at one of their events is a dream come true of every vintner. The other winery owners and I flew there in my plane. I can't tell you how much it means to have exposure to a group of wealthy connoisseurs like…"

Mike interrupted him. "Wait, Mason, the victims were all from those wineries, except for you."

"Yes, Mike, there's the nexus. I am the only vintner from Sonoma who was at the Brotherhood of the Knights of Wine event in Colorado Springs who has not been murdered. Yet."

The three of them were silent, thinking about the implications of what Mason had just said. Ted was the first to speak. "Did anything take place when you were there that seemed suspicious?"

"No. That was also part of my thinking process tonight. I can't recall anything in particular."

"If you don't mind, Mason, let me summarize what you just said. My mind works better that way," Mike said.

"Feel free to. I could probably use a summation as well. My head's been spinning for the last few hours."

"You're saying that you flew the victims to Colorado Springs for this event along with their wine."

"Yes. Correction. My pilot flew them to the event in my plane. Prior to flying to Colorado Springs, each of us had shipped approximately twenty cases of wine to the Broadmoor to use for the tasting. It's a pretty big deal. When people buy cases of wine at these events, the vintners fill the orders when they return home. It would be too expensive to have cases of wine there for them to take with them. The wine that we sent ahead was wine that we would serve at the sampling party which took place after the new members were -

initiated into the Brotherhood."

"Got it. Nothing unusual took place at the event that you're aware of. Is that correct?" Mike continued.

"I know of nothing, and I never heard any of the others indicate that anything unusual or suspicious had taken place while we were there."

"Okay, so about two-and-a-half years after all of you return to Sonoma, Riccardo Neri is murdered and then the other murders took place with the time between each murder becoming shorter and shorter. Is that correct?"

"Yes."

"Mason, are you concerned you might be the next victim?" Ted asked.

In spite of his tan, Mason's face paled. "No. I'm not concerned, I'm terrified. Once I put it all together, I realized I'm the last man standing, and it's not a very happy place to be."

"Mason," Mike said, "the only nexus between the victims that you're aware of is this trip to the Broadmoor. Did that particular group go anywhere else together?"

"No. Certainly we'd get together at the Winery Owners Association meetings and often met each other at one or another's winery, but there were always other vintners there. To my knowledge that is the only time that particular group of people was assembled together with no one else present." He sat back, lines of worry clearly etched on his face.

"Ted, what do you think?" Mike asked.

"I think Mason has come up with more than we have, even though we've been working on this case around the clock, 24/7, since the first murder took place. It looks to me like something happened at the Broadmoor that led to the murders. What happened is the unknown."

"Seems to me someone needs to go to the Broadmoor," Mike said. "Mason, you have a plane. Can you fly my wife and me there tomorrow morning? Ted needs to be here with Alessia and for the funeral. This may take more than a day."

"Yes. I'll call my pilot right now and alert him. I'll also call my assistant and have her make reservations for you at the Broadmoor, as well as arrange for a car to be at the airport. She's been with me for years, and if I tell her that I don't want her to tell anyone about your trip, she won't and neither will my pilot. I'll pick you up tomorrow morning about 7:15. Since it looks like I may be the next planned victim, I'll happily foot the bill for you to go there."

"Mason, that won't be necessary," Ted said. "I have some funds in my office account for things like this. Mike, what about your dog, Rebel? Do you want to take him? I don't know what the Broadmoor's policy is regarding dogs."

Mike took a moment to consider it. "Hadn't even thought of him. I know Alessia's allergic to dogs, so that's not an option. Know of a place where I can board him for a day or two? Problem is he's current with everything, but I didn't bring a record of his shots. Most places that board dogs have very firm policies about a dog being current with their shots and Bordatella vaccine."

"I think I can cover that. Let me make a call." Ted picked up his phone and said, "Hi, Jim. Got a favor to ask. I think you met Kelly Reynolds today. I don't know if you met her big boxer dog, Rebel, but Kelly and her husband, Sheriff Mike Reynolds, are going to Colorado in conjunction with Julie's murder investigation.

"They can't put him in a kennel because they didn't bring his shot record. Any chance you could keep him for a couple of days? You can?" He gave Mike a thumbs up. "Great. Second question. Any chance you could come out to the guest house at the Lugano Winery early tomorrow morning, about 7:00, and pick Rebel up? They're going to be tight on time. Great, they'll see you around 7:00. Thanks, Jim."

He turned to Mike and said, "Okay, that's taken care of. You're flying in a private plane, so you can take your gun. Mason, what time will the plane be ready? Fortunately, there's only a one-hour time difference between the Broadmoor and here."

"I believe it's a little over four hours from here by plane. If you leave at 8:30 in the morning, you'll get there around 1:30, their time. That will give you plenty of time to get to the Broadmoor. What do you hope to accomplish?"

"I want to talk to the events or convention manager and find out what was going on at that time. I'd like to see if they can recall anything unusual. Mason, can you tell me a little about the actual event?"

"Sure. It was very well run. We got there in the afternoon and the welcoming party, induction of new members, and the wine tasting took place that evening. I think it ended around 8:00. We all packed up, got some luggage carts to load up the little wine that was left, and took it to our rooms.

"The following day we attended some morning seminars and then by pre-arrangement, we flew back to Sonoma that afternoon, landing around 7:00 that evening. All of us were happy about our trip to Colorado. It was a huge deal for us to have our wines highlighted at the Brotherhood wine tasting."

"So, as I'm listening to you, I get the feeling that the wines from your group were the only ones being tasted. Is that correct?" Mike asked.

"Yes. We each had a table and signs and promotional stuff that we'd sent to the Broadmoor earlier. All of us had done tastings like that before. The venue provides the wine glasses, table coverings, and whatever else is needed. We provide the wine, our banners, and advertising materials. Even though it's a standard practice at wine tastings, they took it up a notch," Mason said.

"In what way?" Mike asked.

"Usually at events like this, there are a number of vintners. Each one has a table, and they're usually pretty close together. At the Broadmoor, we were in a large outdoor patio area with a huge fireplace, and tall cocktail tables. There were only the five wineries being spotlighted, so there was plenty of space between each vintner's table. That's important because if it's too crowded, a lot of potential customers don't have a chance to sample the wines they want to try and you lose sales."

"And the tasting lasted how long?"

"As I recall, it was from 5:00 to 8:00 in the evening. As I said, there was a welcoming speech, the induction of the new members, and then the wine tasting."

"Mason, this is an event where alcohol is prominent. Is there any self-policing? I guess what I'm asking is what is the protocol if someone becomes intoxicated? And are the number of glasses of wine a person consumes monitored by anyone?"

"Mike, I think at a prestigious event like this, everyone self-polices. Nobody wants to be the person throwing up in the corner of the room. We're all grownups. As a matter of fact, at the really high-end wine tastings, I don't think I've ever seen anyone inebriated. I'm sure some people have too much too drink at these events, but it's not been overt. And no, drinks are not monitored, but keep in mind these are not teenagers trying to see how much they can drink before someone catches them. These are connoisseurs, so they really are far more interested in the quality than the quantity."

"Mike, Mason, excuse me for a minute. I need to make a phone call. I'll be right back," Ted said as he stood up and walked out of the room.

"Yes, I see what you're saying about excessive drinking," Mike said. "It's late, and since I'm leaving early in the morning, I better get going so I can get some sleep. Mason, is there anything else you can tell me either about the victims or the Broadmoor that I should know?"

Mason was quiet for a while and then he said, "No, I can't think of anything else, but if I do think of something, I'll text you. What's your phone number?"

Mike gave it to him. A moment later Ted walked back into the room. "Mason, I've arranged for around-the-clock security protection for you. Rather than using my deputies, I called a friend of mine in Napa who has an excellent security service. A lot of the high-end wineries use his service at their events.

"Since the victims seem to have known the murderer, or at least we suspect they did, one of these guards will be with you at all times. They'll be dressed in street clothes, so they shouldn't draw any attention. They'll sleep in your house, be with you during the day, and wherever else you go. I know it may be inconvenient for you, but I'd rather you were inconvenienced than dead, harsh as that sounds."

"Ted, I couldn't agree more with you, but I'm kind of surprised you didn't use sheriff's deputies. Any special reason why you didn't?" Mason asked.

"Yeah. If it's someone who is known to the vintners, I thought it might be best to keep this very quiet. My deputies are well-known in the Sonoma area and would probably be asked questions, possibly by the murderer. I'd like this aspect of the investigation to be under the radar, so to speak."

Mason gave him a tight smile. "I hadn't thought of that. You're probably right. I'll make sure that even my people don't know who they are. I'll just tell them that I'm helping some people who want to learn more about wine."

Ted turned to Mike. "Mike, on that same note, I'm not going to tell anyone that you've gone to Colorado or why. I'm going to say that you had to leave unexpectedly due to an emergency back in Cedar Bay. Since Rebel will be staying at Jim's, I'll likewise alert him not to say anything to anyone. If one of his staff asks why Rebel is there, he can just tell them that he's keeping him because a friend of his had to go away unexpectedly."

"Good idea, Ted," Mike said. "That makes a lot of sense."

"Ted, when will the guard be at my house?" Mason asked.

"He won't be going to your house initially. I told my friend to have the first shift come here to my house, so he can escort you home and spend the night. He'll be here in about half an hour. From then on these security guards will be with you in eight-hour shifts around the clock."

"Given that schedule, it's probably a good thing I'm not married," Mason said, smiling for the first time that evening. He turned to Mike, "I hope you find out something in Colorado."

"You're not the only one," Mike said as he shook his hand. "Stay safe tonight. See you in the morning. Ted, I'll check in with you and let you know what I find out. Try and get some sleep. The next two days are probably not going to be easy for you, what with the funeral and post-funeral reception."

"I will, and Mike, I'm really glad you're here to handle this. I couldn't do this on my own."

"Happy to help," Mike said as he walked out the door. He just hoped he was able to deliver.

CHAPTER TWENTY

When Mike got in bed a little later that evening, he pulled Kelly towards him and said, "Honey, wake up. I need to talk to you. No problems, just a change in plans."

Kelly woke up with a start. "Mike, what's happening?"

"Before I tell you, how did you do that?" He looked at her in amazement. "You're came alert instantly."

"Comes from years of being a mother. You learn to wake up fast when a child cries out or has a nightmare. Now tell me about the change in plans."

Mike told her about his meeting with Mason and Ted, and that they were flying to Colorado Springs the next morning and would be staying at the Broadmoor and why.

She listened and then asked, "What about Rebel? Are we going to take him with us?"

"No, we thought it would be better if he stayed here, given that we don't know what the pet policy is at the Broadmoor. Fortunately, Jim, Ted's nephew, said he'd be happy to keep him while we're gone. I would have considered boarding Rebel at a kennel, but we don't have his shot record with us, and I doubt if we could get him in anywhere tonight or that early in the morning. Jim's coming by at 7:00 tomorrow morning to get him. He'll be fine."

"What are you going to tell Alessia? She'll wonder what's happened to us. And remember, I was supposed to help her tomorrow."

"I was thinking about that on my way back from Ted's. I believe the best thing to do is say that something came up in Cedar Bay, and I had to get back to take care of it. Naturally you're coming with me. The way Alessia's house is situated, we'll be able to load Rebel in Jim's van, and she'll never know about it."

"Why aren't you going to tell her the truth?" Kelly asked, confused.

"Kelly, more and more the evidence, what little there is, actually let's say the way the murders have occurred, is leading us to believe that all of the victims were acquainted with the killer. If that's true, and it seems to be based on the lack of struggles or any DNA evidence under the victim's fingernails which would indicate resistance, then the murderer very likely could be someone from the Sonoma area.

"If the wine tasting event at the Broadmoor was the trigger point or the beginning factor that led to these murders, and the person hears that someone who is investigating the murders has gone to the Broadmoor, the killer might think they were about to be discovered and would try to escape. If everything seems to be normal, and our leaving because of an emergency certainly is, their suspicion that we're getting closer to identifying them won't be aroused. If anything, it would be the opposite."

"How long are we going to be gone? And don't forget, Julie's funeral is the day after tomorrow."

Mike stroked her hair. "I don't know if we'll make it back in time for the funeral. It all depends on what I find out when we get there. If we do come up with something solid while we're there and then we come back here, it might be better for us to take the lowest profile possible. In other words, not be seen. Kelly, this is all conjecture. Right now, everything is very fluid. We'll just go from point A to point B and see what happens. Okay with you?"

"Do you even need to ask? Of course. I'll be with you every step of the way."

"Thanks. Let's get some sleep. Who knows what tomorrow will bring?"

CHAPTER TWENTY-ONE

The next morning, Kelly had just finished packing when she heard Jim's van drive up. Mike was already outside and motioned for Jim to park on the far side of the house out of view. He came back in the house, got Rebel, put him in the van along with his food and dog bed, and moments later they were off, no one being the wiser.

"Mike, have you seen Alessia this morning?" Kelly asked, while she wheeled the suitcases to the front door.

"I did. She was walking out of the house with the vineyard manager to look at some vines he thought might be having a problem. I told her that there had been an emergency in Cedar Bay, and we were leaving. I told her how sorry we were to have to miss Julie's funeral, and I hoped she understood. I also apologized for you not being able to help her today."

"What did she say?"

"She understood. Business is business whether it's the wine business or law enforcement business. She told me to thank you again for giving Casey to her. He was right next to her when she headed out, and he looked very content. I think that was a very good match."

"Good, I'm glad." She glanced away and said, "Looks like our ride to the airport is here." A moment later a large black Mercedes Benz pulled up in front of them. Two men got out of the car and walked towards the trunk.

Kelly walked towards them and said, "Hi, I'm Kelly, Mike's wife. One of you must be Mason."

Mason smiled at her and said, "That would be me, and this is my friend, Chris."

"It's nice to meet both of you. Mason, Mike speaks highly of you, and I want to thank you for flying us here and now flying us to Colorado Springs."

"Pleased to meet you, Kelly. But I'm the one who should thank you for spending your vacation time here in Sonoma trying to help Ted, and since I'm probably the next intended victim of the Wine Country Killer, I'm especially appreciative." He turned to Mike and said, "Good morning, Mike, about ready to go?"

"I am. Let me help you with these suitcases. Kelly, would you go back inside and see if we've missed anything?"

"Yes, I need to get my purse and my iPad. Be right back."

A half four later Mason pulled up in front of his plane at the Napa airport. "Plane's been checked out and the pilot is ready. I think you can take off a little earlier than what we talked about last night. I hope you find something relevant, and that this isn't some wild goose chase. I had fresh coffee and sweet rolls put on the plane for you. Have a safe trip, and I'll look forward to seeing you when you return."

The pilot waved to Mason and walked down the stairs to get Kelly and Mike's luggage. He looked at Kelly and said, "Where's that big beautiful boxer? Does this mean he won't be flying with us?"

"It does. He had to stay in Sonoma, but he'll have plenty of canine company, so I think he'll be happy," Kelly said. Mike and Kelly followed him up the stairs, turned, and waved once more to Mason and Chris and then walked into the luxurious plane.

"Kelly, fasten your seat belt. You've got nothing to do for a few hours but read that book you've been working on. I'm probably going to use this time to get some sleep. I want to be at my best this afternoon, and if needed, tomorrow."

Moments later they were in the air, bound for Colorado Springs, hoping to find answers to unsolved murders.

CHAPTER TWENTY-TWO

"Mike, wake up." Kelly shook him by the shoulder. "We're getting close, and we should be landing pretty soon. You have to see the Rocky Mountains. This is really something."

Mike yawned, stretched, and then looked out his window. "I agree. That's spectacular." Doing a double-take he added, "I'm kind of surprised to see that much snow on them."

"While you were taking your shower this morning, I did a quick search, and there's snow on them even in the summer. Of course, a lot of it melts, but not all of it. This is a first for me. I've never been to Colorado, and I've always wanted to go there. And did you know that the Broadmoor was originally a dairy farm and then it was converted to a luxury hotel? That was about one hundred years ago. As a matter of fact, I found out it's the longest consecutively running Five Star, Five Diamond hotel in the United States."

"You're quite the font of knowledge this afternoon. And no, I didn't know any of that."

"Yep. Matter of fact a lot of presidents and other heads of state have stayed there. They have over seven hundred seventy-five rooms, three golf courses, and all kinds of restaurants and shops. You should have brought your golf clubs."

"Probably should have, but even if I had I rather doubt I'd have time to play. Looks like we're landing. Got your seat belt on?"

"Yes, safety sucker," she said in a teasing voice. "I'm legal. Not to worry."

When they'd landed and the plane had come to a stop, a black SUV pulled up next to the plane followed by a sedan. Kelly and Mike were walking down the steps of the plane as a man walked up to them.

"Mr. Reynolds?" the young man asked.

"That's me. Is this the car that was rented for us?"

"Yes, sir. Here's the key. I'll ride back to the rental office with him," he said gesturing to the sedan that was parked behind the SUV. "Please call this number when you know the time and day you'll be leaving. You can leave the car in one of the marked stalls over by that building," he said as he motioned towards a nearby hangar. "Just leave the key under the mat on the floor. One of our staff will pick it up."

"How shall I pay you?" Mike asked.

"That's already been taken care of, sir. Mr. Bryant gave us a credit card number to use. Hope you enjoy your stay here in Colorado Springs." He walked over to the second car, got in, and waved as it drove away.

The pilot carried their luggage down the stairs and put it in the back of the SUV. "Mr. Reynolds, I'll be staying here in Colorado Springs until you're ready to leave. Here's a card with my cell phone number on it. Mr. Bryant would like you to call me and let me know when you want to leave. The plane and I will be waiting for you. Enjoy your stay. I'll see you soon."

"Thanks, Captain. That was a very smooth flight. It was so smooth, I slept most of the way."

"Glad to hear it, Sir," he said as he walked back up the steps of the big jet.

They climbed into the SUV, which had the new car smell Kelly wished came in an aerosol can, because she'd always found it impossible to replicate. Mike checked his mirrors before they set off. "Ready, Kelly? Mason gave me directions on how to get to the Broadmoor from here. Looks like it will take about twenty minutes or so, although I wouldn't mind just staying here and soaking up this view," he said as he looked at the nearby mountains.

"From what I saw on the internet this morning, the view from the Broadmoor is even better. Let's go."

Twenty minutes later they saw several pink stucco buildings connected on a circular path around a lake. "Mike, the article I read said that it was built like the grand hotels on the coast of the Mediterranean in an Italian Renaissance style. Look how the buildings blend into the landscape."

"Makes me wish we were here for a different reason, like just enjoying ourselves on a vacation. I'm making a mental note to myself to come back and do just that. As hard as we both work, we deserve it."

"You won't get an argument out of me. I'm sorry we're here under these circumstances, but I have to say I'm not sorry we're here."

Mike stopped at the valet stand in front of the hotel and told the valet who had opened his door, "We'll be staying here, so you can take our luggage out of the back and park the car." He gave the attendant his name and the key and then they walked into the grand old hotel.

A few minutes later, Mike held out his hand to take the envelope containing the key cards to their room from the young woman at the registration desk. "Sir, here's a map and how to get to your cottage. It's on the 18th green of the East Golf Course and has a beautiful view of Cheyenne Mountain. I think you'll enjoy it. Is there anything else I can help you with?"

"No, actually yes. Could you arrange for our luggage to be taken to the cottage?"

"Of course, Sir. Enjoy your stay and please let us know what we can do to make it more pleasurable for you."

"Okay, Kelly, this way," Mike said as he walked away from the registration desk.

"Mike, she said a cottage, didn't she?"

"That's what the lady said. This should be interesting. I was expecting an ordinary hotel room. Guess not."

A few minutes later they walked up to their cottage and saw that a cart with their luggage was in front of the door. The bellman opened the door and motioned for them to precede him into the room. He followed with their luggage, set it down, and immediately started a fire in the fireplace.

"May I do anything else for you, Sir? Would you like some ice?"

"No, this is fine," Mike said as he took his wallet out of his pocket and gave the young man a tip. "Thank you."

"Please call if you need anything," the bellman said as he left and closed the door behind him.

Mike looked over at Kelly whose eyes were as wide as saucers. She let out a squeak. "Mike, this is unbelievable. I've never stayed anywhere like this. We should have brought Julie, Brad, and the girls. They'd love it here. And that view. Even the bathroom is incredible. It looks like a spa. How did we ever get something like this?"

"Mason said his assistant would arrange everything. Looks like she did a beautiful job. Of course, Mason was the one who gave them instructions for the type of accommodations he wanted us to have. When we get back we need to give him a huge thank you. Then again, if we find out who the murderer is and save his life, that will probably be thanks enough."

"Where are you going to start?" she asked.

"With the event manager. I'll play it by ear after that."

"I'll unpack while you call. So far, I've seen four phones, so take your pick," she said with a laugh.

Mike sat down at the desk and pressed the button for the front desk. "Could you connect me with the events office? Thank you." A moment later Kelly heard him say, "This is Mike Reynolds. I'd like to speak to the Events Manager. Yes, I can hold."

She walked into the bedroom to hang up the few clothes they'd brought and couldn't hear Mike's end of the conversation. A few minutes later she walked back into the room and asked, "Were you able to set up a meeting?"

"Yes. I, actually we, have a meeting with Jason Mangers at 4:00 this afternoon."

"Did he ask what it was about?"

"No, but I told him. I thought it might save time if he could pull up whatever information he might still have about the Brotherhood event that was held here three years ago."

"Good idea. Mike, we haven't eaten anything other than a sweet roll on the plane. Why don't we go to the coffee shop and get a sandwich? I think we both need to be at the top of our game for this meeting and if we're starving, that's bound to affect us. I don't want either of us to miss something important."

Mike checked his watch. "You're absolutely right, and we've got just enough time. You need a few more minutes or are you ready to go now?"

"I'm ready," she said as he picked up his briefcase and they left the cottage. "Mike, I think it may be a good thing Rebel didn't come with us."

"Why would you say that?"

"Well, we're on the 18th hole of a golf course, and I can see golf balls on it right now. If Rebel was here, he'd probably think it was some kind of a game and run out and get them. I don't think the golfers here would be very happy if that happened."

"I think he's getting a little old to do something like that, Kelly, but it just might make him revert to his puppy days. Anyway, you're right about getting something to eat. Glad you suggested lunch. I'm starving."

CHAPTER TWENTY-THREE

Promptly at 4:00 that afternoon, Kelly and Mike opened a door that had the words "Events Manager" in brass letters on it.

"Hi, I have an appointment with Jason Mangers at 4:00. My name is Sheriff Reynolds," Mike said to the woman of an indeterminate age sitting at the desk in the waiting room. He looked over at Kelly and winked, sure she'd know what he was thinking.

The woman looked like she had been put in the office by someone who had just seen an old "schoolmarm western" movie and decided to cast a receptionist as a prim woman from the middle of the 19th century.

She wore a long-sleeved buttoned-up white blouse, large tortoiseshell glasses with a chain hanging from them, and her hair was pulled back in a severe bun. There was not a trace of make-up on her face and a yellow pencil was stuck in her hair above her right ear.

Kelly winked back acknowledging she knew what he was thinking. A moment later the woman said, "Go down the hall,ir. Mr. Mangers' office is the second door on the right."

As they were walking down the hall, Mike said in a low sarcastic tone, "She kind of made me feel all warm and fuzzy. Did she do the same for you?" Kelly responded by lightly swatting him on the arm.

He knocked on the door and a moment later it was opened by a tanned middle-aged man who looked like he skied in the winter and spent the summer fishing in the nearby lakes and streams. In contrast to his skin, his teeth looked even brighter than they already were. "You must be Sheriff Reynolds. I'm Jason Mangers. Please, have a seat," he said as he and Mike shook hands.

"Thanks for taking the time to meet with me, Jason. This is my wife, Kelly."

"Welcome to the Broadmoor, Mrs. Reynolds." When they were seated he said, "You mentioned that you wanted to talk to me about the Brotherhood of the Knights of Wine event that was held here at the Broadmoor three years ago. I pulled the file for you and made copies of everything that was in it for you, but I didn't see anything unusual. I'm assuming since you wanted to see me regarding it, that there was something out of the ordinary that occurred during the event. What am I missing?" He handed the file to Mike and sat back.

"Jason, I don't know what I'm looking for. That's why I'm her." Mike spent the next twenty minutes telling Jason in detail everything that had happened from the first murder of Riccardo Neri to the murder of Julie Lugano. Then he told him about his meeting the night before with Mason Bryant and the nexus of the Brotherhood event.

When he was finished, Jason said, "I can certainly understand why Mr. Bryant is concerned, but I can't think of anything that occurred that evening that would lead to or include murder. I was personally present at that event and saw nothing unusual.

"I remember the Brotherhood event quite well because it was the first event I did here at the Broadmoor. I'd only been on the job a week. When I heard that the Events Manager job was open I applied for it and was hired. I had previously been working at a similar job in Denver, but I love to ski, hunt, and fish, so this job here at the Broadmoor is a dream come true for me." His teeth dazzled when he smiled. "Anyway, I wanted to make sure everything went well, so I personally supervised every last detail of the event."

"Can you think of anything or anyone that seemed the least bit out of the ordinary to you?" Kelly asked.

"Not a thing. The people I dealt with from the Brotherhood were very professional. They hold events like this twice a year, and they knew exactly what they wanted. Actually, it was one of the easiest events we've ever put on. No drama or problems at all, which is unusual. I wish I could be of help, but I really don't know anything more to tell you.

"About the only thing I remember from that night is feeling great about how well it went, and then getting stuck in a major traffic jam for an hour on my way home. Believe me, that was not the way I was planning on celebrating my first event at the Broadmoor."

Mike stood up and said, "We won't take up any more of your time. I really appreciate your meeting with us. I'll take a look at the file, but from what you're saying, it looks like this is a dead end." He and Kelly walked toward the door.

"Nice meeting you, Sheriff. Funny, I haven't thought about that night for a long time. I remember being so happy with the way the event had gone, and then having that feeling disappear the longer I waited in that traffic jam."

"Ever find out what the traffic jam was about?" Mike asked as he put his hand on the doorknob.

"I remember wondering if there would be anything on the late news that night and turning on my television when I got home. A woman and two young children were killed by a hit and run driver. Since I'd kind of been affected, I followed the case, but they never did find the driver. Guess it was just one of those things."

"They happen," Mike said. "Again, thanks for your time."

"No problem. Enjoy your stay," Jason said as he closed the door behind them.

"Speaking of events," Kelly said. "That was kind of a non-event, and I'm sorry for Mason or whoever is footing the bill for this expedition into the unknown. Looks like it was a wild goose chase."

"Agreed. Let's go back to the room and decide what we're going to do for dinner. I probably need to call our pilot and tell him we'll be leaving tomorrow morning. Okay with you or do you want to stay longer?"

"No, might as well get back to Sonoma and see if we can find some clue working from that end of things. Alessia will probably need some help tomorrow afternoon after the funeral and everything else."

CHAPTER TWENTY-FOUR

"Mike, let's have dinner at The Summit restaurant," Kelly suggested, having checked out the dining options. "It's part of the Broadmoor, and I looked at the menu on the internet this morning. I think we'd really like it. This is their nod to Pike's Peak. Okay if I call and make reservations?"

"Sure. Kelly, did anything stand out to you about our meeting with Jason?"

She thought for a moment and then she said, "Not really. About the only thing I came away with was how sad it is when a mother and her two children are killed and someone leaves the scene of the accident. And then they can't find the person responsible for it."

"That's stayed with me too. I have a hunch that has something to do with everything, although I have nothing to base it on. As long as I'm here I'm going to call the chief of police in Colorado Springs and see if we can get an appointment with him tomorrow morning. I'll hold off calling our pilot until I talk to him."

Kelly went into the bedroom to make their dinner reservations while Mike called the police station. When she walked back in the living room, he was on the phone.

"Any chance you could schedule me for an appointment with him for tomorrow morning, say, around 9:00? I'm leaving town tomorrow afternoon, and I'd really like to talk to him before I leave. As I mentioned before, it's about several murders that have occurred in Sonoma, California."

He looked at Kelly and made a motion with his index finger indicating he wanted the person on the other end of the line to hurry up. "We can see Chief Lynn then? That's great. What's your address?" He wrote down the address and ended the call by saying, "I really appreciate your help, Rosa. See you tomorrow morning." He ended the call and looked at Kelly. "Guess you heard that."

"Good. It's kind of like a loose string hanging. When we leave, at least we'll feel that we followed up on everything we could. You have an hour to relax before our reservation."

"Think I'll read the file Jason gave me. That way, if I have any questions I can call him from here, rather than Sonoma."

*****

They walked into the Summit Restaurant promptly at 7:00 and were immediately seated at their table. "When I saw that crowd of people around the hostess stand, I figured we were in for a long wait," Kelly said. "Glad to see they honor reservations."

She looked over at him and said, "Mike, this is delightful. Quite different from the restaurants we've eaten in the last two nights. I love the way it's designed with the interplay of wood, metal, glass, leather, and even the table fabrics." She fingered the cutlery— chunky, heavy silverware. "It's modern and elegant in its own way, but not the least bit pretentious. I think we're in for a good experience."

He looked at his menu, and then said, "I never order anything like this, but I'm going to start off our evening with a drink called the Sparkling Summit. I have no idea what most of the things in it are, but it sounds interesting, and you?"

"Seriously? Cap Rock gin, yuzu, honey, cherry herring, and topped with bubbles? Don't expect to have one of these when we get back home. I think I'll stick to something I know, like a glass of red wine."

Their waiter appeared a moment later, took their drink orders, and said he'd return in a few moments with them. They were quiet as they read over their menus.

"Mike, what looks good to you?"

"Everything, but I think I'll hone it down to the Summit Caesar salad and the bison tenderloin. I love a good Caesar, and I've never had bison. And you?"

"Lobster bisque and since we're kind of doing a Colorado theme, I'm going to have the braised Boulder natural chicken à la Basque. Kind of a 'when in Rome, do as the Romans do' thing."

When they'd finished their entrees, the waiter returned and said, "Here is the dessert menu. Do you have any questions?"

"Only one," Kelly said. "What is your favorite dessert on the menu?"

"My favorite is the pumpkin cheesecake. It's quite different from usual cheesecakes with the cinnamon ice cream, but I think you'll like it."

"You sold me. Mike?"

He looked up at the waiter. "Please bring us two forks. I'll try a couple of bites of hers."

"Certainly, sir."

"I couldn't recreate that if I tried for the rest of my life," Kelly said a little later, pushing her plate away, "but I enjoyed every bite."

"May I bring you some coffee or a glass of port to end your

meal?" their waiter asked a few moments later.

"No thank you," Mike said. "I'm full and tired. You can bring the check."

"Yes, sir."

CHAPTER TWENTY-FIVE

"Good morning," Mike said to the police department receptionist. "I have an appointment with Chief Lynn. My name is Sheriff Reynolds."

"Have a seat, sir. I'll tell him you're here."

Mike and Kelly sat down on two of the wooden chairs that lined the nearby wall. Both of them got out their phones and were looking at their emails when a large man with salt and pepper hair and a mustache walked over to them. "Hi, I'm Chief Lynn. You must be Sheriff Reynolds," he said as he extended his hand to Mike.

Mike and Kelly both stood up and Mike shook his hand. "I'm Mike and this is my wife, Kelly."

"It's nice to meet both of you. Let's go back to my office," he said as he opened a door and motioned for them to follow him.

"Please have a seat. What can I do for you, Sheriff Reynolds?"

"I really don't know. Here's the situation." Mike told him about the Sonoma murders, their trip to the Broadmoor, and then the offhand remark Jason had made about a mother and two children who had been killed in the parking lot of a McDonald's restaurant by a hit and run driver.

"Okay, Mike, I have the picture. What do you want from me?"

"I'd like to know if you ever found the driver who ran over and killed those three people. I'm clutching at straws here, Chief, but I'm wondering if there was anything that linked their deaths to the Brotherhood of the Knights of Wine or the wine tasting that night." He held up his hand as if forestalling what Chief Lynn was going to say.

"I know this sounds really way out there, but they did occur on the same night. Can you think of anything?" Mike asked.

"First of all, Sheriff…"

"Please call me Mike."

"Okay, Mike. Let me begin by saying I was not the chief then. As a matter of fact, I was the police chief in Durango, Colorado, so I have no personal knowledge of the case. If you'll give me a minute, I can pull the file up on my computer and see if there's anything that might be of interest to you."

"Thanks, I'd appreciate that."

When he'd had a chance to scan the file, he turned to Mike and said, "There's nothing I can see that would link the victims of the hit and run to the Brotherhood or the wine tasting that took place at the Broadmoor that night. The driver was never caught. We did locate an abandoned rental car in the parking structure at the Broadmoor that had front end damage on it as well as blood stains on the right front fender. The blood stains matched the blood type of the deceased hit and run victims.

"The car had been rented by an individual by the name of Ethan Morris. We checked with the airlines in Denver and discovered that a person by that name was listed on the passenger manifest for a flight from Denver to Mexico City several hours after the hit and run occurred. We worked extensively with the police authorities in Mexico trying to locate Mr. Morris, but he was never found. There is an assumption that he was the hit and run driver.

"Based on probable cause that he was the driver, we got an arrest warrant issued by the local court and filed it with the federal immigration authorities, requesting that a hold be placed on this guy Morris if he ever tried to re-enter the United States. That hasn't happened, and I rather doubt it ever will."

"Sounds like it's a dead end as it relates to Morris," Mike said.

"Sorry, Mike. I know you were hoping for more, but that's all I've got."

"I don't have my file with me. It's back at the Broadmoor in my room, but for some reason that name rings a bell. Who was the chief before you?" Mike asked.

"That would be Chief Robertson. He was a great chief, but he developed Parkinson's disease and had to take an early retirement."

"Does he live in Colorado Springs?"

"Yes. As a matter of fact, I go over there about once a week for lunch. We've become very good friends. His daughter is divorced. She lives with him and pretty much runs his ranch. He has mobility problems and spends most of his time in a wheelchair, but his mind is as sharp as a tack."

"I'd like to talk to him about the case. Maybe he remembers something that wasn't put in the file. Could you give me his telephone number?"

"Sure," Chief Lynn said. "He was a very active man, so being tied pretty much to his house and being in a wheelchair is very hard for him. I think he'd love a chance to revisit a case. Here's his number." Chief Lynn wrote it down on the back of his business card and handed it to Mike. "When you see him, tell him I'll be there next week at the usual time."

The three of them stood up. "Chief, thanks for your time. I have no idea if there's a connection between the hit and run driver and the murders in Sonoma, but I'd be remiss if I didn't follow even the slightest hint of a lead."

"That sheriff in Sonoma is lucky to have someone like you helping him. Hope I can call on you if I ever need some help."

"Put me up at the Broadmoor, arrange for a game of golf, and I'll do whatever you need," Mike said with a laugh as he and Kelly walked out of the chief's office.

"Now what?" Kelly asked.

"I want to go back to the cottage and look at the file Jason gave me. I'd swear I saw Ethan Morris' name on the list of names of the people who attended the Brotherhood event. After that I want to call Chief Robertson and see if I can set up an appointment with him."

"Looks like we won't be going back to Sonoma today. I wonder how Rebel is doing? I hope he's okay."

"Don't worry. He's probably having a wonderful time with the other dogs. Who knows? Jim just might teach him a trick or two," he said as they got into their car.

"Rather doubt it. Think there's a reason for the saying, 'You can't teach an old dog new tricks,' at least I haven't had much luck in the last couple of years."

"That's probably why you own a coffee shop and you're not a dog trainer," Mike said.

Kelly fastened her seat belt. "You're probably right."

CHAPTER TWENTY-SIX

"Kelly, I was right," Mike said, pointing to the file. "Ethan Morris' name is on the list of members who attended the Brotherhood of the Knights of Wine event. As a matter of fact, he was installed as a new member that night."

Kelly looked up from her iPad. "Well, that's interesting. Are you assuming he was the hit and run driver?"

"Absolutely, and the local police think the same thing. They even got an arrest warrant issued for him."

"Let me play devil's advocate for a moment. He may be the hit and run driver who killed a mother and her two children in Colorado Springs, Colorado, but what does that have to do with the Sonoma murders?"

"At this point I have no idea, but maybe Chief Robertson can help me with that. I'm going to call him now and see if we can meet him this afternoon. Okay with you?"

"Sure, I'm just along for the ride."

"Right. Like you've never been an integral part of some of my murder investigations in the past," he said with a chuckle.

"Well, now that you put it that way, I may have helped you a time or two."

"Or three or four…"

"And that. Call the chief while I go outside for a moment, look at Cheyenne Mountain, and just breathe in this great mountain air. It has a ton of health benefits, you know, including weight loss. High altitude decreases the appetite by making you feel full longer. In fact, Colorado has the nation's lowest obesity rate, according to Dr. Google. I'm hoping it takes affect right away."

When she returned a few minutes later Mike said, "Kelly, Chief Robertson said he'd be happy to see us. He asked what it was about, and I told him. He said he remembers the hit and run case well because it was one of the major cases still unsolved when he left the department. We're meeting with him at 2:00 this afternoon. That will give us time for lunch. Okay with you?"

Kelly nodded. "Sure. Does he live nearby?"

"No, he said he's about half an hour from here. Evidently, he inherited a little ranch from his father and like you heard earlier, he and his daughter live there."

*****

Mike followed the chief's directions and turned onto a road that led up to a sprawling one-story ranch house with a large barn behind it. "Mike, this is like something out of a movie. I mean there's the traditional white fence and horses in the pasture on the other side of it. It's beautiful. I wonder who cares for all of it?"

"Don't know, but we'll find out soon enough." He parked in the circular driveway in front of the house. "He must have a lot of help to keep the ranch in such great condition. Quite frankly, given the nature of his disease and the fact he's a retired city employee, I was expecting somewhat of a ramshackle place."

As soon as they reached the top of the steps, the door opened and a woman who appeared to be in her late thirties greeted them. "Welcome to the Robertson Ranch. I'm Amelia Robertson. Dad's expecting you. Follow me. He's in his study."

They walked down the hall and Kelly couldn't help but look in awe at the furnishings and decorative objects in the house. On the hall wall were a number of paintings of horses with brass plaques mounted on the paintings' frames indicating each was a winner in a race at a certain racetrack, many of which were familiar to Kelly because they were so famous.

A booming voice greeted them as they walked into the study. "Welcome. I'm Matt Robertson. You must be Sheriff Reynolds and this must be Kelly," the man in the wheelchair said. Twinkling blue eyes assessed them, and having passed some test that only Chief Robertson had the key to, he said, "You're wondering how an old man who has Parkinson's disease and is a retired city employee can afford all of this. Would I be right?" He made a broad gesture with his hand.

Mike grinned and said, "I've been told never to lie to the police, so the answer is yes."

"Sit down. Amelia, how about getting a glass of iced tea for our guests, and I'd take one too. Thanks." He turned to Mike and said, "My father was a real estate developer in Colorado Springs and did quite well. He bought this ranch and started raising thoroughbred horses. When dad became involved in something, he went all out. He got the best trainers and horses money could buy, and his horses did very well."

"I noticed the paintings in the hall as we were walking down it. I assume those are all horses from your ranch," Kelly said.

"You'd be right. When dad died I inherited the ranch and continued to breed, train, and race horses. They still do well. I can't travel to the different racetracks, but I have a state-of-the-art video system that allows me to see my horses in real time as they race, no matter where in the United States the race is being held. And it goes without saying that I have a ranch manager who is excellent. For what I pay him, he should be.

"Amelia helps me with anything that has to do with the horses. She's a natural with them. Seems to be in her blood. After her divorce, I asked her to come here to live and told her I'd pay her a salary to help run this place. It's worked out well. She has her suite of rooms on the other side of the house, and I have mine. I have round-the-clock help for me as well as a cook, a maid, and groundskeeper. Obviously, we have a lot more help for the ranch and the horses. We get by."

"From the looks of it, you're getting by very well," Mike said with a laugh.

"Been lucky, Mike. Been lucky, even with this disease. The doctors tell me its progressing very slowly, and that's a good thing. Now, what can I do for you?"

Mike spent the next half hour telling him everything that had led him to this moment including the information about Ethan Morris. "What I'm asking, Matt, is if there's anything you can remember about the case that wasn't in the file. I'm hoping since you were the chief when this went down that something will come to mind. I honestly don't know what I'm looking for."

Matt was quiet for several moments. "I've been thinking about it ever since you called, and it is the one case that still stays with me. The tragedy that wasn't in the file is that the woman and children who were killed were the wife and children of one of my best officers. He personally took over the investigation of the case. I really didn't want him to because I felt he was too emotionally involved, but he convinced me he was going to do it anyway on his off time, so I let him do it.

"He said he wouldn't be able to live with himself if he didn't devote every minute of his life to it. Something that never got into the file, because it was simply a hunch on my guy's part, is that he was sure alcohol played a part in the death of his wife and children. He found out that Ethan had attended the Brotherhood of the Knights of Wine event at the Broadmoor, and he was sure Ethan must have been drinking."

"Interesting. I just found that out, and I think I'd probably have to agree with him, but I understand that Ethan was never found," Mike said.

"That's true. Mexico and the United States have an extradition treaty that was signed in 1968, but you have to find a person before you can extradite them. My guy tried everything and never found Ethan. He even went to Mexico City where Ethan had evidently fled on the night of the hit and run, but couldn't turn up anything. It's still an open case, but I don't think Ethan will ever be found. Really, Mike that's all I know, and unfortunately, I don't think it will help you with the Sonoma murders."

"No, it doesn't. Well, you were my last chance. Think it's time to go back to Sonoma with my tail between my legs. Thanks for your hospitality and please thank your daughter for the iced tea. Kelly, we probably need to call our pilot and tell him we'll be leaving in the morning."

They stood up and walked to the door. "Oh Matt, I just thought of something. Is that policeman whose wife and children were killed still on the force? Maybe I should talk to him."

"No, Kevin resigned. He told me if he couldn't find the person who killed his wife and children, he wasn't a very good policeman, and it was time for him to leave the force…"

Mike spun around and walked back to where Matt was sitting. "Matt, what's his last name?"

"O'Reilly. Kevin O'Reilly."

"Mike, that's the name of the sheriff's investigator who's in charge of the Wine Country Killer murders, isn't it?" Kelly said, her heart starting to race.

"Yes, Kelly, you're right. Chief, I need two things. I need to see a photograph of this man, and I need to know if your police department was ever contacted by the Sonoma Sheriff's Department as part of a background check on him."

"Mike, I don't like the sound of this." Matt's brow furrowed. "Tell me, do you know if your Kevin O'Reilly is a teetotaler? I ask because in a place like Sonoma it would be kind of strange not to drink wine, and the Kevin O'Reilly who worked for me became somewhat of a fanatic about drinking after the accident. He joined a number of organizations that are against alcohol. I mean he really went off the deep end. He refused to touch one drop of alcohol, and before that he used to love a beer or two."

"I don't know, but I can find out. Let me call Sheriff Dawson and see."

"While you're doing that I'll call Chief Lynn and see if the department received a background request concerning Kevin. I'll also ask him to scan a photo of Kevin and send it to me as an email attachment."

Mike pressed Ted's telephone number into his cell phone. "Ted, I'm sorry to bother you, but I have an odd request, and it's connected to the murders. Do you know if Kevin O'Reilly drinks alcohol?" He waited a moment and then said, "He told you he had a personal reason for not drinking? Did he tell you what it was?"

Mike listened and then he said, "So you don't know what it was. What do you mean it doesn't matter?" He listened again and then said in an urgent voice, "Double Mason's guards. Do it immediately. I can't explain now. I'll get back to you in a few minutes."

"Mike, Chief Lynn said there was a routine request from the Sonoma Sheriff's Department over two years ago regarding Kevin O'Reilly," Matt said. "He was given a very favorable reference, and that was the end of it. Here's his photo on my computer screen."

Kelly walked over to it and gulped. "That's him."

Mike looked over Kelly's shoulder and said in an urgent voice, "Kelly, call our pilot and tell him to be ready to leave in an hour. We've got to get back to Sonoma as fast as possible." He turned to Matt and said, "Kevin called Ted, the Sonoma sheriff, a little while ago and said a personal matter had come up, and he was resigning his position with the sheriff's department effective immediately."

"What do you think that means, Mike?" Matt asked.

Mike exhaled loudly. "I think he's the killer, and he's going to finish off the last vintner, Mason Bryan, by murdering him tonight. In his mind he will have avenged the deaths of his wife and children by murdering the last of the vintners who provided wine to Ethan Morris, the man who killed his wife and children."

"I think you're right Mike. Let me get someone from the police department to go to the Broadmoor and get your things. I'll have them taken to the airport. It will save you about half an hour. I just hope you get there in time."

"Thanks, Matt," Mike said as he and Kelly hurried out of the house. "Kelly, you drive. I need to call Ted and tell him what's happened. Mason has to keep to his normal schedule, so Kevin isn't alerted that we're on to him."

He called Ted and they devised a plan, hoping against hope that they weren't too late.

CHAPTER TWENTY-SEVEN

Mike and Kelly raced to the airport where they hurried up the steps of the plane and were met by the pilot. "Your luggage was delivered by the police and is already loaded. I have clearance, and we're ready to go. Sit down and buckle up. Kelly told me it was an emergency, so I'll get us there as fast as I can. The sheriff called and said he'd be waiting for you when we land." He quickly turned and walked into the cockpit.

"Mike what do you think?"

"I'm sure we have our man. I just hope we get there in time to save Mason. From what Tim said, Mason has a regularly scheduled meeting with his vineyard manager every Thursday night at 9:00. That means Kevin will know exactly where Mason will be tonight at 9:00."

"That's kind of weird. Why not during the day?" Kelly asked.

"Mason felt that they could both give their full attention to any problems with the winery or in the vineyards if they didn't have other people around. It has the same feel that each of the other murders had. All of the murders occurred when they did certain things at certain specific times, and this fits right into his pattern."

"You know, Mike, I kind of understand why he committed the murders. I'm not saying that's right, and of course it's not, but…"

"I know, Kelly, I've had the same thoughts. He had the three people he loved more than anything else in the world killed by someone who had too much to drink and he couldn't bring the murderer to justice, so he did the next best thing, at least in his mind. He decided to kill the people he thought were responsible for the man having too much to drink. Not that any of them forced him to drink the wine."

"Mike, what are you going to do when we get to Sonoma?"

"Ted is meeting me at the airport. He's rented a car. His sheriff's car would be too conspicuous no matter where we parked it. By the way, he'll have Rebel with him, but Rebel will come with me. A sheriff's deputy will take you to the guest house. I'd like you to take our luggage. I'll be there when I'm finished."

"Finished with what?" Kelly asked.

"I don't know."

*****

The sky was just starting to turn a deep shade of blue when the big jet taxied to a stop at the airport in Napa. There was a sheriff's car and a sedan waiting for them on the tarmac. Mike waved goodbye to Kelly as he hurriedly got into the sedan and was immediately greeted by a very excited Rebel.

"I'm glad to see you, too, big guy," he said to Rebel, "but stay in the back seat while I talk to Ted." He turned to Ted, "I'm sorry to take you away from Alessia and whatever else you had planned for this evening, but I really think Kevin is the murderer. And how convenient that he's been the lead investigator in the Wine Country Killer case, so if there were any clues, he could easily dispose of them."

"Yes, ever since you called, naturally I've thought of nothing else," Ted said. "I'm sure it's him. I'm kicking myself for not checking into his background more thoroughly, but I finally convinced myself there

131

were no signs that would have led me to do it."

"You can't blame yourself. As I told you when I called, the murders committed by the Wine Country Killer were a result of a man leaving the country and going into hiding. Unfortunately, the vintners were innocent victims just as Kevin's wife and children were innocent victims. To change the subject, Mason has no idea we're coming, right?"

"That's right. I told Mason we were doubling up on security as a standard precaution. He asked if you'd found out anything, and I told him you called and said we'd talk when you got back to Sonoma. He doesn't suspect a thing."

"Good, because I don't want him to change his schedule. That might alert Kevin. Here's what I think we should do." He told Ted his plan.

Shortly before 9:00, Ted parked his car several blocks from the entrance to the winery, so it simply looked like the car had run out of gas. Ted quietly whispered to Mike, "Think someone is looking out for us because it's a very dark night with almost no moonlight. There's a small one-room building over there, Mike. That's Mason's office and it's where he meets his manager. They share a glass of wine and talk. Mason told everyone that since it was good enough for his dad, it's good enough for him."

"Alright," Mike said, "here's what I think we should do. See that tree over there, a few feet from the front door? I'm going to hide behind it with Rebel. It's dark, so we won't be seen. You go around to the side of the building where I can see light coming from that window. Stand out of the light, but be ready to shoot through it if need be. Wish us luck."

As Mike and Rebel made their way towards their hiding place behind the tree, Mike passed close by one of the windows of the small building. He quickly glanced inside and saw that Mason, his manager, and the two security guards that Ted was providing for Mason's protection, were all sitting at a table in the room. Mike and

Rebel quietly moved on to their hiding place behind the tree and waited. They didn't have to wait for long.

Twenty minutes later Mike saw a shadow moving towards the front door of the building. It was Kevin O'Reilly. Mike put his hand on Rebel's head to calm him, sensing the tension in the dog. When Kevin was at the front door Mike stealthily walked behind him. As Kevin pulled out his gun and was in the process of opening the door, Mike yelled at Rebel, "Attack legs."

Kevin whirled around as Rebel hurled his big frame at Kevin's knees and legs, causing him to fall backward into the building's small room. His gun went off in a wild shot. Mike yelled, "Don't move. Rebel, stand guard." The big dog held Kevin down while Ted ran around from the side of the building and grabbed Kevin's gun which was laying on the floor next to him.

"What the…" Mason said pushing his chair back from the table where he'd been sitting, as the two security guards hurried over to Kevin, their guns drawn.

"It's your lucky night, Mason," Mike said as he kept his gun trained on Kevin. "The man who murdered the other vintners was the lead investigator trying to catch the Wine Country Killer. It's ironic, but they were one and the same person, and your instincts were right. You were scheduled to become his final victim tonight. Ted, call a couple of your deputies and have them come and get Kevin."

"Kevin, while we're waiting, why don't you tell us about the murders? Save everyone a lot of trouble," Mike said.

"I have nothing to say other than how did you know it was me?"

"I think you just said a lot, Kevin," Ted said. "You have four guns on you, so I'm going to suggest that Mike command his dog to get off your chest, but I strongly suggest you don't move. Be a shame if one of these guns accidentally went off, especially if it was my gun. I could always claim self-defense, and when I think of Julie, I might be persuaded to do it. And I'd be willing to bet these men would back me up."

"She deserved it. She was just like the others," Kevin yelled. "Serving too much wine to rich people, and one of them got drunk and killed my wife and children. Julie got what was coming to her and so did the rest of them."

The room was soon lit up with flashing blue and red lights from two sheriff's cars that came to a screeching stop next to the front of the building. The deputies threw open their doors and ran into the small building.

"Boys, cuff him and take him to the station," Ted said to them as he pointed at Kevin who was still lying on the floor.

"Sir, he's one of ours. That's Kevin O'Reilly," one of the deputies said.

"Good notice. Kevin's also the Wine Country Killer. I'll be at the station in a little while. Now get going and be sure and read him his Miranda Rights, because I think he's going to sing like a bird."

CHAPTER TWENTY-EIGHT

"Mike, every time I think back to what happened in Sonoma, I still can't believe you were able to solve the case and capture the killer," Kelly said a few weeks later as she was fixing dinner.

"You're not the only one. I think what still amazes me is why I ever asked Matt what the policeman's name was. If I hadn't done that Mason would be dead, and Kevin would have gotten away with it. A split second earlier and we would have walked out of there, none the wiser."

"Well, I'm sure you're a hero to all of the Sonoma vintners, and remember, Mason did tell us we have a standing invitation to stay at his winery whenever we're in the area. And I haven't told you yet, but he sent us a case of his best reserve wine. I think we're set for months."

"That was a nice gesture, but I guess that's what vintners do when someone saves their life."

"Mike, have you talked to Ted lately? I know you were talking to him pretty regularly for a few days after Kevin was arrested."

"Yes. I'm pretty sure I'll have to go back to Sonoma to testify at Kevin's trial. Ted said my personal testimony would be needed if Kevin's attorney isn't able to negotiate a plea bargain with the

District Attorney. I'll just have to wait and see what happens."

"Does that mean we'll get to fly in a private jet again? Probably too much to ask Mason if we could go to the Broadmoor again?"

"I think that would be pushing it, Kelly. Between the private plane trips, the Broadmoor, and the dinners in Sonoma, someone spent some serious money on us."

"Have a feeling that given he's still alive, Mason would say it was the best investment he ever made," Kelly said.

"You're probably right. By the way, Ted is selling his house and moving into the guest house at the Lugano Winery. Alessia said she would really like his help in running the winery. He said he'd lost the fire in his belly for ferreting out the bad guys after one of his own officers killed the woman he was going to marry. I feel really bad for him, but it does look like he's getting on with his life, and that's a good thing."

"Agreed. Did he say anything about his nephew, Jim, and Casey?" Kelly asked with an innocent wide-eyed expression on her face.

"Come to think of it he did. He mentioned that Jim was spending a lot of time at the winery helping Alessia train Casey."

"I knew it, I just knew it," Kelly said with a smirk on her face.

"Knew what?" Mike asked.

"That there was a spark between them."

"You're reading way too much into that. He's just a dog trainer helping someone with a dog he trained."

"Mike, you may be a great sheriff, but when you retire don't try to make it in the matchmaking business. Murder clues are no problem to you. Relationship clues are a huge problem. Just mark my words. We'll be getting a wedding invitation within the year."

"You think?" Mike asked with a shocked expression on his face.

"Sure do, Sheriff. Now go open one of those bottles of wine Mason sent us, and we'll toast the happy couple prematurely."

"Make you a bet. If you're right you have to pay for a trip to the Broadmoor for us. If you're wrong, I have to pay for a trip to the Broadmoor for us. Deal?"

"Sounds like a win-win. You got yourself a deal, Sheriff."

RECIPES

COFFEE CAKE MUFFINS

Ingredients:
Muffins:
1 ½ cups all-purpose flour
1 tsp. baking powder
1/8 tsp. baking soda
1 cup sugar
½ cup unsalted butter, room temperature, cut into small pieces
2 jumbo size eggs
½ cup sour cream
1 tsp vanilla extract (Don't use imitation.)
12 cup muffin tin
Topping:
½ cup firmly packed brown sugar
½ cup all-purpose flour
½ tsp. ground cinnamon
½ cup cold unsalted butter, cut into pieces

Directions:
Topping:
Preheat the oven to 400 degrees. Put brown sugar, flour, and cinnamon in food processor and pulse to combine. Drop the butter on top and pulse until the mixture begins to form pebble-like

nuggets.

Muffins:

Put flour, baking powder, baking soda, and sugar in a food processor and pulse 3 times. Sprinkle the butter over the dry ingredients and pulse until the mixture is the size of small peas. Add the eggs, sour cream, and vanilla. Process for 30 seconds.

Scrape down the sides of the bowl and pulse until the batter is blended. Scoop ¼ cup of the batter into each muffin cup and top with 1 tbsp. of the topping. Bake until golden and a skewer inserted into the center comes out clean, 15 to 17 minutes. Serve and enjoy!

SALMON PASTA WITH CREAMY GARLIC SAUCE

Ingredients:
4 oz. fettucine
½ lb. fresh salmon fillets, preferably skinless
Dash of onion powder
Salt and freshly ground pepper to taste
1 tbsp. olive oil
1 tbsp. butter
½ cup dry white wine
1 tbsp. fresh lemon juice
¾ cup heavy whipping cream
1 shallot, minced
3 cloves garlic, minced
½ cup grated Parmesan (Don't use canned Parmesan.)
1 tbsp. flour
1 tbsp. fresh basil leaves, minced

Directions:
Cook pasta in large pot of water according to package directions. Drain, reserving 1 tbsp. water. Season salmon lightly with onion powder, salt, and pepper.

Put olive oil and butter in a large skillet over medium high heat.

When hot, add the salmon. Cook for 2 minutes on each side. Remove salmon from pan and set aside. See note below if skin is attached to fillet.

Add white wine, lemon juice, cream, garlic, shallot, and Parmesan to the skillet. While stirring, scrape the bottom of the pan so the brown bits get incorporated into the sauce. Slowly add the flour to the sauce, constantly stirring to avoid having lumps.

Add the salmon back into the skillet and break it up with a cooking spoon, so it's reduced to bite-size pieces. Gently mix into the sauce. Cook for an additional 5-6 minutes until the salmon is cooked through and sauce is thickened. Add cooked and drained pasta to skillet, along with reserved water. Gently mix the sauce and pasta. Serve and scatter with basil. Enjoy!

NOTE: If the salmon fillet has the skin attached, after the fillet is removed from the skillet, peel the skin off with your fingers. Once the skin is removed, using a thin metal spatula, scrape off the dark material that was under the skin.

ITALIAN SALAD

Ingredients:
Dressing:
½ cup olive oil
¼ cup mayonnaise
¼ grated Parmesan cheese (Don't use canned.)
1 tbsp. sugar
1 tbsp. vinegar
2 tsp. freshly ground black pepper
1 clove garlic, pressed
Juice of one lemon
Optional: 1 tbsp. chopped fresh basil, oregano, thyme, or rosemary

Salad:

1 head romaine lettuce, roughly chopped
½ head iceberg lettuce, roughly chopped
6 pepperoncini, diced
½ cup whole red cherry tomatoes
½ cup red onion, thinly sliced and chopped
1/3 cup grated Parmesan cheese

Directions:

Put the dressing ingredients into a blender and blend.

Put the romaine and iceberg lettuces in a large bowl and toss with the dressing. Top with pepperoncini, olives, tomatoes, and onions. Sprinkle with Parmesan cheese. Serve and enjoy!

PORTUGUESE SEAFOOD STEW

Ingredients:

16 oz. can crushed tomatoes
2 lb. russet potatoes, peeled, and cut into 2" chunks
1/3 cup olive oil
½ tsp. red pepper flakes
5 garlic cloves, minced
2 medium yellow onions, roughly chopped
2 bay leaves
1 medium red or orange bell pepper, cored, seeded, and roughly chopped
1 cup bottled clam juice
½ cup dry white wine
18 fresh mussels, rinsed and debearded (You can substitute clams.)
2 lb. boneless, skinless cod filets, cut into 1 ½" chunks
3 tsp. minced fresh cilantro
Kosher salt and fresh ground pepper, to taste

Directions:

Bring a large pot of salted water to a boil. Add potatoes and cook until tender, stirring occasionally, about 15 minutes. Drain and set aside.

Heat the oil in a large pot over medium high heat. Add tomatoes, red pepper flakes, garlic, onions, bay leaves, bell pepper, and cook about 15 minutes, stirring often. Add clam juice, wine, salt, and pepper. Cook for 5 minutes, stirring occasionally. Add mussels or clams and cover pot. Cook until the shellfish just begin to open, about 4-5 minutes. Add fish and continue to cook, covered until all shellfish are opened and the fish is cooked through, about 5 minutes more.

Transfer fish stew to a large serving bowl and sprinkle with ½ of the cilantro. Place the potatoes in another serving dish alongside stew, sprinkle with remaining cilantro and enjoy!

NOTE: If any of the shells on the mussels/clams don't open, they should be discarded.

VANILLA BEAN FLAN WITH CARAMEL SYRUP

Ingredients:
Syrup:
1 ½ cups sugar
½ cup water
Flan:
1 ½ cups half and half
1 ¼ cups heavy whipping cream
1 cup sugar
1 ½ vanilla beans, split lengthwise
1 ½ cinnamon sticks
Peel from 1 ½ lemons, removed in strips with vegetable peeler
3 jumbo size eggs
4 large egg yolks
Optional Garnish: 3 large oranges, all peel and pith removed

Directions:
Syrup:
Position rack in center of oven and preheat to 350 degrees. Arrange eight ¾-cup custard dishes on work surface.

Please sugar in heavy medium skillet. Shake to even thickness. Cook over medium heat without stirring until sugar starts to dissolve, about 5 minutes. Using a wooden spoon, stir until all sugar is dissolved and syrup turns a deep amber, about 5 minutes longer. Add ½ cup water (mixture will bubble up). Simmer until caramel is smooth and thickened, stirring constantly, 1-2 minutes. Evenly divide caramel into custard dishes.

Flan:
Combine half and half, cream, and sugar in large heavy saucepan. Scrape seeds from vanilla beans and add to mixture. Add cinnamon sticks and lemon peel. Stir over medium heat until bubble form at edge of saucepan and sugar is dissolved. Set aside to steep for 15 minutes.

Whisk eggs and egg yolks in large bowl to blend. Gradually whisk in warm cream mixture. Strain flan into a bowl, then divide equally among the caramel-lined custard dishes. Place cups in roasting pan. Add enough hot water to roasting pan to come halfway up sides of custard dishes.

Bake flans until just set in center, about 35 minutes. Transfer to large rimmed baking sheet. Chill in refrigerator uncovered until cold, then cover and chill overnight.

Cut around each flan with a think knife to loosen. Turn out with caramel syrup to plate. If desired, cut between the membranes of the oranges and garnish with orange segments. Enjoy!

COMING SOON!

PUBLISHING 12/4/18
MURDER IN THE CAYMAN ISLANDS
BOOK NINE OF
THE NORTHWEST COZY MYSTERY SERIES
http://getBook.at/CI

The latest in the nine book Northwest Cozy Mystery Series by a two-time USA Today Bestselling Author.

Things aren't always what they seem. What could go possibly go wrong on a vacation in the Cayman Islands? After all, everyone knows it's a tropical haven in the Caribbean with beautiful women, plenty of rum, mouth-watering seafood, duty free shopping, and some of the best scuba diving and snorkeling in the world? Well, murder for one.

When DeeDee, Jake, Al, and Cassie go to Al's home in the Cayman Islands for a respite from the string of murders they've had to investigate in the last year, the last thing they expect is to be involved is yet another murder. And it's even harder when it's Al's longtime Mafia friend and next-door neighbor, Nicky Luchesse.

There are plenty of suspects including islanders, old Mob acquaintances, and a couple of women the murderer knew very well. The problem is, they all have a motive, but which one committed murder?

Open your smartphone, point and shoot at the QR code below. You will be taken to Amazon where you can pre-order 'Murder in the Cayman Islands'.

(Download the QR code app onto your smartphone from the iTunes or Google Play store in order to read the QR code below.)

ABOUT THE AUTHOR

Dianne lives in Huntington Beach, California, with her husband, Tom, a former California State Senator, and her boxer dog, Kelly. Her passions are cooking, reading, and dogs, so whenever she has a little free time, you can either find her in the kitchen, playing with Kelly in the back yard, or curled up with the latest book she's reading.

Her award winning books include:

Cedar Bay Cozy Mystery Series

Cedar Bay Cozy Mystery Series - Boxed Set

Liz Lucas Cozy Mystery Series

Liz Lucas Cozy Mystery Series - Boxed Set

High Desert Cozy Mystery Series

High Desert Cozy Mystery Series - Boxed Set

Northwest Cozy Mystery Series

Northwest Cozy Mystery Series - Boxed Set

Midwest Cozy Mystery Series

Midwest Cozy Mystery Series - Boxed Set

Jack Trout Cozy Mystery Series

Coyote Series

Midlife Journey Series

Red Zero Series

Black Dots Series

Cottonwood Springs Mystery Series

Newsletter

If you would like to be notified of her latest releases please go to www.dianneharman.com and sign up for her newsletter.

Website: www.dianneharman.com,

Blog: www.dianneharman.com/blog **Email:** dianne@dianneharman.com

Made in the USA
Monee, IL
22 July 2023